OPERATOR 5:
REVOLT OF THE LOST LEGIONS

SECRET SERVICE #5™
OPERATOR 5
AMERICA'S UNDERCOVER ACE

REVOLT OF
THE LOST LEGIONS

By Curtis Steele

POPULAR PUBLICATIONS • 2022

CHAPTER 1
OPERATOR 5 TAKES A HOSTAGE

I T WAS the hour just before dawn. The long gray staff car drove swiftly across the Delaware River Bridge from Camden to Philadelphia.

The wind howled down the river, whipping sheets of rain gustily athwart the bridge, and settling the thickly swirling clouds of mist that are an almost nightly phenomenon in the vicinity of Philadelphia.

But the driver of that car stared grimly ahead, peering out through the rain-sweated windshield, keeping his eyes steadily upon the white line in the center of the bridge, dividing the right and the left-hand lanes. That white line was the only thing visible through the fog. He was dressed in the field uniform of a captain of Intelligence in the Imperial Army of the Purple Empire—the army which had marched irresistibly across America from the Atlantic to the Pacific, conquering the country in the short space of ten months in spite of the desperate resistance of the American Defense Forces.

Now, if it were daylight, and if the fog were to lift, there would be visible, from this point on the bridge, the flag which flew over the Philadelphia City Hall—the flag of the Purple Empire upon which was emblazoned the symbol under which the goose-stepping Purple troops of Emperor Rudolph I had waged their war of ruthless conquest over two thirds of the earth's surface.

1

Alongside the driver sat a smaller person, wrapped in an auto robe, over the edge of which there showed a pert young nose and a hint of blonde, ringleted hair. As the wind whipped the robe aside, there was revealed at times a youthful face, apparently that of a girl of perhaps fifteen or sixteen.

The hundred Americans of the Suicide Squad rushed the pill-box.

The Captain of Intelligence drove with the swift, sure efficiency of a man to whom the handling of automobiles is almost second nature; and he seemed supremely contemptuous of the possibility of skidding on the slippery roadway.

As they neared the Philadelphia end of the bridge, he spoke to his companion. And, surprisingly enough for an officer of the Purple Empire, he spoke in English.

"There'll be a guard at this end," he said. "Remember your lines."

He had hardly finished when a hoarse challenge sounded in the darkness. He slowed down gradually, skillfully avoiding a skid; and his headlights picked out the figures of two troopers of the Purple Empire, barring the roadway with fixed bayonets.

As he brought the car to a standstill, a Purple Empire corporal picked aside the curtain of the open car, stuck his head in, and clicked on a flashlight with which he bathed the faces of both occupants. The corporal's suspicious eyes studied the frowning features of the Intelligence Captain, then he switched to the partly exposed face of the young girl.

"Your pardon, my Captain," he said in the guttural language of the Purple Empire. "You will be good enough to show your credentials." He spoke with just enough of the respect which the strict discipline of the Purple Armies required of its non-commissioned officers, yet there was a certain firmness in his voice. "I regret to stop Your Excellency on such a night, but we have our orders. None must pass here without the proper credentials." The Captain of Intelligence glared at the corporal, seemed about to give way to an outburst of anger, then shrugged. "It is well, Corporal. One must always obey orders." He withdrew from an inner pocket of his tunic a leather case such as was carried by all officers of the Purple Empire, and flipped it open.

The card, under a cellophane window in that case, stated that the bearer was Captain Hugo von der Sturm, of the Imperial Intelligence Service, detailed to special duty. The corporal nodded. "That is well, Your Excellency. And now, as to your companion—"

"This young lady," the Captain said sternly, "is the daughter of His Excellency, Baron Julian Flexner, the Prime Minister to His Imperial Majesty, Rudolph I. I am conducting her to the city for the ceremonies which are to take place there later today."

The corporal was satisfied, and apologetic. "You will forgive me, sir, for having detained you. But orders have been very strict—"

The captain waved aside his explanation. "I understand thoroughly, Corporal. You are merely obeying orders. But perhaps you will tell me the cause of this strictness? Why should you stop a staff car to investigate its occupants?"

The corporal was glad of the opportunity to explain. "You see, Your Excellency, our Commandant, General Count von Folda, has received word that the American spy, Operator 5, is traveling about in this district, accompanied by that brat who is known as Tim Donovan. Operator 5 is said to be disguised as an army officer, and we have been instructed to question all officers, and to report every case where the credentials are not entirely satisfactory. Of course, when such a distinguished young lady as the daughter of Baron Flexner is concerned, there will be no need of reporting. You are free to proceed, sir!"

Captain Hugo von der Sturm nodded genially. "I suggest, Corporal, that in future, when you question the occupants of a car, you do so with your revolver in your hand. I hear that this Operator 5 is a dangerous man."

The corporal shrugged. "We would nab him, sir, be sure. I

have five men here, and if he were in a car, he could not escape."

The girl said nothing, but she looked intensely interested. The captain laughed. "I wish you all the luck in the world, Corporal. I understand there's a large reward upon the head of Operator 5."

"Indeed, yes, sir. To the one who captures Operator 5, His Imperial Majesty has promised the governorship of a whole province in any part of the Occupied Territory of America."

"I hope you get the reward, Corporal."

Captain von der Sturm returned the corporal's salute, threw the car into gear once more, and set it in motion as the guards, responding to an order of the corporal's, stood aside in the roadway.

AND JUST at that moment the powerful headlights of another car, coming from Philadelphia, bathed them in merciless glare, and the roar of a wide-open motor came to their ears. The car stopped with a screeching of brakes, ten feet beyond the corporal's guard, and facing at such an angle that its lights continued to focus on the staff car of Captain von Sturm and his young companion.

Those headlights blinded them all, and Captain von Sturm's eyes narrowed. He nudged his companion, stopped the car.

The corporal said: "*Ack!* It is our commandant, General Count von Folda. He is a martinet for discipline. He makes the rounds personally, twice every night. You will have to answer to him now, sir!"

A deep-throated voice from the newly arrived ear barked: "Stand to attention! Inspection!"

The corporal's guard of five men stopped in the road, presenting arms. The corporal himself stiffened, faced the car, and saluted punctiliously.

Captain von Sturm, peering into the glare of the headlights, was able to distinguish the lines of an open staff car, similar to the one he was driving—with this difference, that two troopers sat in the rear seat, crouched over the sights of the machine gun that was mounted there.

This much he saw before the driver of the car with the machine gun switched off his bright lights, leaving the driving lights to glow faintly by comparison.

A big, heavy-set man with an imperial moustache descended to the roadway. He was dressed in the field uniform of a major-general of the Imperial Army. This would be General Count von Folda—the Commandant of the Occupied Territory of Pennsylvania.

Von Folda barked: "Corporal! Your report!"

The non-commissioned officer spoke respectfully, still standing at salute. "No suspicious persons have passed here tonight, Herr General. All those crossing the bridge showed proper credentials. There was no one who might have been Operator 5."

Von Folda grunted. "And this car—who are its occupants?"

"It is Captain Hugo von der Sturm, Herr General—He is escorting the niece of Baron Flexner into Philadelphia."

"Captain Hugo von der Sturm? I do not know him. Let him step forward. I did not know that Baron Flexner's niece was coming here tonight!"

The corporal turned toward the car of Captain von der Sturm. "You heard, sir, what the General said? Please to speak with him."

Captain von der Sturm seemed strangely reluctant to step out. He hesitated, whispering swiftly out of the corner of his mouth of his companion. The girl nodded her head, which was almost entirely covered by her robe.

General von Folda growled: "Hurry, hurry. Step out quickly!"

Captain von der Sturm glanced up at the two troopers manning the machine gun, shrugged, and opened the door. He stepped out to the roadway, saluted von Folda.

"My respects to the Commanding General," he said. "I am Captain Hugo von der Sturm, of the Imperial Intelligence, escorting the niece of Baron Flexner into Philadelphia."

Von Folda stared at him suspiciously. "I will speak with the young lady. I know her." He stepped forward, pushing the corporal and young von der Sturm out of the way, and leaned in at the open door of the car.

"We cannot be too careful," he started to say, by way of grudging apology. "There is a very cunning American spy abroad tonight. He poses as a Purple Empire offi— *Gott im Himmel!*"

The last words were wrenched from von Folda's lips as he froze in petrified astonishment at sight of the demure looking young lady in the car, who was calmly and deliberately pointing a heavy revolver at his head!

UNDER THE headlights of the general's car, the young lady's action could be plainly seen by the troopers at the machine gun, as well as by the corporal and his guard in the road. But the machine gunners dared not open up, for fear of hitting their own commandant.

It was an arresting tableau there under the beating rain and the whipping wind. Five rifles of the guards in the road were raised, with bayonets gleaming in the headlights; machine gunners in the general's car crouched over their weapon, awaiting a chance to shoot; and the corporal tense, with his hand on his holstered gun, glaring at the girl in the car.

She did not seem disturbed by all this display of hostility. For a tenderly nurtured girl of fifteen, she appeared quite cool under the menace of those guns. And her voice, strangely like that of a boy rather than a girl, sounded clearly in the night above the whistling of the wind. She spoke in English, without the slightest hint of accent—which was strange for a daughter of the Purple Empire.

"Stand still, General von Folda. If you move, I'll shoot your teeth through the back of your head!"

Von Folda exclaimed: "This is not Freda Flexner! I know the daughter of Baron Flexner—And I do not understand her. She speaks English—"

Young Captain von der Sturm, standing close beside him, had drawn his own revolver, with which he covered the corporal. He smiled tightly, his eyes grim. He interpreted his companion's words, speaking in the language of the Purple Empire—"She says, my dear General, that it would be bad for your health to make a move against us. As you see, your men could not fire upon us without hitting you; while either of us could easily shoot you down. Now, will you do us the honor to step into our car, General?"

Von Folda spluttered in futile rage: "W—what is the meaning of this? W—who are you? You are no Imperial captain; and this is not Flexner's daughter—"

"Very clever of you to have guessed it, General!" young Captain von der Sturm raised his eyebrows. His voice lost its geniality, became crisp, businesslike. "Get into the car at once!"

Von Folda started slowly to obey.

Out of the corner of his eye, Captain von der Sturm saw that one of the troopers in the general's car had picked up a rifle, and was taking careful aim at the befurred figure of his young companion.

The trooper's finger was already contracting on the trigger, and young von der Sturm thrust General von Folda out of the way, raised his revolver and fired, almost in the same motion. The heavy slug caught the trooper in the chest, hurled him backward out of the car.

But the damage was already done. Von Folda had gone staggering under the young captain's thrust, slipping on the wet road, and he careened into the corporal. Now, both the general and the corporal were out of range of the gun in the hands of the befurred figure in the car, and they were also out of the line of fire of the machine gun.

The second trooper at the machine gun bent to the trip. In

an instant he would spray the captain's car with a hail of lead, cut down both of them.

Captain von der Sturm's eyes were grim as he swung his gun slightly, fired once more. The second trooper screamed, fell away from the machine gun, with blood spurting from his left shoulder.

The troopers in the road rushed in toward the car, bayonets gleaming, while von Folda, struggling to his feet, shouted hoarse commands to them: "Take them! Take them! It is Operator 5!"

Captain von der Sturm leaped to the running board of the car. "Get going, Tim!" he shouted to his companion.

His command was unnecessary. The befurred figure of the girl had already slid over into the driver's seat, and, while von der Sturm fired over the windshield at the advancing troopers, the car leaped into motion, drove straight at the gleaming bayonets. The troopers shouted in alarm, jumped to one side to avoid the roaring automobile.

From behind them, General von Folda was firing his revolver at the two fugitives, his face red with rage. The corporal had leaped to the general's car, and swung the machine gun around, bent over the trip. The machine gun began to chatter its deadly *rat-tat-tat,* and whining slugs slapped the air around the fleeing car.

OPERATOR 5, *alias* Captain von der Sturm, had emptied his revolver. While his companion, with blonde hair streaming in the wind, kept the car roaring away toward Philadelphia, he reloaded with desperate swiftness, while slugs from the machine gun screamed in his ears. Then, leaning far out from the side of the car, holding on precariously with one hand, he fired back deliberately at the corporal, who was stooping over the machine gun.

The general's car had turned and was coming after them, with von Folda himself standing beside the corporal and holding the belt that fed cartridges into the breech.

The night became discordant with the chattering of the machine-gun, the shouts of the troopers, the deep-throated roar of Operator 5's revolver, and the spiteful bark of the troopers' rifles, all mingling with spattering rain and the raging wind howling down the Delaware.

The fleeing car hurtled onto the long ramp of the bridge, leading into the heart of Philadelphia. It was gaining on the pursuers. The first burst of machine-gun fire had been wide, and the pseudo daughter of Baron Flexner was driving a reckless zig-zag course, thus making of themselves a very difficult mark. The tires skidded on the wet ramp, and she barely brought the car back under control, exhibiting amazing skill for a girl.

But the skid had lost them their advantage. The bursts of machine-gun fire were coming closer now, and Operator 5 reloaded his revolver once more. "More speed, Tim!" he shouted. "They're gaining on us!"

"I can't get any more speed out of this can, Jimmy. My foot's almost pushing through the floorboards now!"

Operator 5 raised his gun again, took careful aim. They were almost out of revolver range of the pursuers, but the Purple Empire troopers had rifles and the machine gun. They could still reach the fugitives, and a lucky shot might hit a tire or the gas tank. That would be disastrous anywhere, and more so here, on the slippery ramp. The canvas top of the car was already ripped and gaping in a dozen places. Slugs were tearing in through the back, but they were traveling upward at a slight angle, otherwise they would have smashed in the back of the driver's head. It would not be long before the corporal at the machine gun succeeded in lowering his sights.

Operator 5 braced himself on the running board, with the wind tearing at his back and rain beating against him. He slowly and carefully sighted his revolver at the left side of the windshield of the pursuing car, and shouted to his driver: "Slow up, Tim. I want to get back in range!"

The blonde-tressed driver nodded, and deliberately let up on the gas, though the slugs from the pursuing machine-gun were slapping uncomfortably close. The distance between the two cars diminished perceptibly, and Operator 5, aiming carefully emptied his gun into the windshield of the General's auto.

There was a scream of terror, heard above the cacophony of shots and storm. The pursuing car swerved, slid, and then skidded half-way around, smashing into the railing of the ramp, breaking through and catapulting over the side toward the ground far below.

A sheet of flame burst from the falling car, and a uniformed figure leaped wildly out, to somersault through the air. In a moment the general's car crashed to the street below, a flaming mass of wreckage.

Operator 5 sighed, holstered his gun, and climbed back into

the car, beside the driver. "That's that, Tim," he said. "It was a hell of a thing to do—but war is hell, anyway!"

The young driver kept the wheel steady, eyes forward on the road ahead. "Gosh, Jimmy—" huskily—"are—are they all dead?"

"Every one of them, Tim. Even the troopers. They all piled into the car after us."

"Then—then there's no one left alive who knows that you're Operator 5—and that I'm Tim Donovan!"

"Right, Tim. We can go ahead with our mission. Keep that blonde wig on—straighten it out. It's come askew in the excitement."

He reached over and held the wheel while Tim Donovan straightened his wig, wrapped the fur more tightly about himself. Then the boy took the wheel again, drove off the ramp and swung to the right, into Vine Street.

THIS BOY who was disguised as a girl was the sixteen-year-old Tim Donovan—the lad who had been the almost constant companion of Operator 5 during the latter's Herculean efforts of the last ten months to stem the tide of the Purple Invasion.

Operator 5 was no more than a number in the secret records of the United States Intelligence Service. But though he was still a comparatively young man, he had made that number almost a legend. In the far places of the world, when men rested from intrigue and adventure, they spoke with bated breath of some of the exploits of Operator 5; and before the Purple Invasion, no foreign country had ever dared to launch a campaign of espionage in America—without first considering the possibilities of meeting the opposition of Operator 5.

He, together with his Chief—the man known as Z-7—had for years successfully maintained an insuperable wall of counterespionage against the machinations of spies and saboteurs.

But that had all been before the Purple Invasion. Operator 5 had foreseen the menace of Rudolph's Empire. He had watched the Dictator of the militaristic country of Balkaria rise to the position of Emperor; had seen the Purple Empire spread its field of conquest over Europe and Asia, and he had constantly urged that the United States prepare for defensive war. But his warnings had gone unheeded, and the Purple Emperor strengthened his empire, threw every resource into the manufacture of war material of the most advanced kind.

When the Purple Legions at last landed in Canada, marching south along the eastern seaboard of the United States, American defenders found their equipment was like a child's toys compared to the long-range cannon, the highly-mechanized infantry, and the modern battle planes of the invaders.

The goose-stepping troops of the Purple Empire, commanded by the veteran Marshal Kremer, moved inexorably inland, burning, ravaging, pillaging, torturing and killing. In spite of courageous resistance and heroic sacrifice, flesh and blood could not stand against steel and powder. The Imperial Armies swept across America to establish a new empire for Rudolph I.

And through it all, the only effective opposition had been led by Operator 5 and a small band of devoted followers. That opposition had enabled the American Defense Forces to slow up the Purple Invasion by several months, but could not stop it. Now,

The pursuing car skidded, smashing into the railing.

with America under the heel of the tyrant conqueror, Operator 5 was still planning, scheming, fighting to drive the invaders out.

To the small circle of followers who knew and loved him, he was not Operator 5—he was Jimmy Christopher, warm-hearted, considerate, generous. To his Imperial Majesty, Rudolph I, self-styled Emperor of the World, his name was anathema; for he had successfully outwitted the cleverest generals, diplomats

and spymasters of the Purple Empire, and was still at liberty. Rudolph knew that if America ever succeeded in driving his goose-stepping troops out of the country, it would be due to the leadership of Jimmy Christopher.

The Emperor had made prisoners of two of Operator 5's band—big, hearty, Aloysius MacTavish, one-time sergeant of the Canadian Mounted Police, and Jimmy's own twin sister, Nan Christopher, Those two were awaiting death in New York. And Operator 5, moving with swift desperation, was now in the process of carrying out a plan to save Nan Christopher and Sergeant MacTavish.

But even with his twin sister under the shadow of the executioner's rope, Operator 5 still carried the welfare of the country in his heart. The plan to save his sister was inextricably bound up with another plan, to strike a blow at the invaders. How well those two plans would work would be revealed by the events of the next few hours. Just now, on the bridge, he had almost met with disaster at the hands of General Count von Folda. During the next few hours he and Tim Donovan would be risking their lives again and again—and the least slip would mean failure and death. Yet neither hesitated.

TIM DONOVAN drove swiftly westward along Vine Street, against the one-way signs. Vine was a one-way street, eastbound, but the traffic rules did not apply to staff cars of the Purple Empire.

There were no lights anywhere in the city. No American civilians dared show themselves, or show a light in their houses at this hour. The curfew laws were strict, punishable by instant death—or worse. No one in the streets after six o'clock; lights out at seven— those were the rules. And they were enforced strictly, gleefully, by the sadistic subordinates of a sadistic emperor.

The squalid tenements of this district were dark, somnolent in the early morning hours. Not before eight o'clock would they ordinarily come to life, for that was the hour when the curfew law permitted civilians to emerge from their homes.

Twice Tim Donovan slowed up as they passed patrols of Purple Empire troopers, prowling the streets with ready rifles. But as soon as the troopers saw the insignia of the Purple Empire on the side of the staff car, they saluted and allowed them to pass.

That insignia was the dread emblem of the severed head and the crossed broadswords, under which the Purple Emperor had conquered two thirds of the earth's surface. Grimly, the promise of that emblem was carried out by the wholesale executions of civilians in the Occupied Territory; and the headsman's axe was ever red with the blood of men and women who died to satisfy the vengeful zest of Rudolph.

Tim Donovan drove quickly through the Chinatown district, then swung into the Parkway leading into Fairmount Park. The once beautiful park grounds were now nothing but a vast stretch of seared tree-trunks and pitted ground. This whole park district had been subjected to intense drumfire during the advance of the Purple troops, and a bloody battle had taken place here, with the Americans fighting every inch of ground. Fairmount Park was now only a forgotten wilderness, with here and there the rotting bones of dead soldiers. Forty thousand men had perished in the Battle of Philadelphia, and most of them had died here. After the Purple troops had taken the city, American civilians had been compelled to work on the battlefield dumping the bodies of their friends and relatives into the Schuylkill River. They had buried many of them, furtively, but had left many others. The stench here was almost intolerable, and few people ever frequented the site of the park with its scenes of misery and desolation.

But Tim Donovan and Operator 5 seemed to know where they were going. The boy drove on, over pitiful remnants of road, past the wreckage of the Art Museum, then turned left toward the bank of the Schuylkill.

Here along the edge of the River was a long row of deserted shacks that had once been boat houses. Those shacks now seemed dark, deserted and ominous, but Tim Donovan drove purposefully toward them.

The going was rough here, because of the shell-scarred terrain, and the lad had to slow up almost to a crawl. And while they were still several hundred feet from the row of shacks along the river bank, they began to hear curious sounds. From the right came the eerie hoot of an owl, while a wildcat screeched on the left.

And suddenly, dark figures emerged on all sides of the car, from behind tree-stumps and dead clumps of shrubbery and from out of shell-holes. Ominous, dark figures, that moved with stealth and silence, surrounding the staff car. Knives gleamed in the night, and the dull sheen of revolver barrels glinted.

Lithe forms pressed close on both sides of the auto, and guns were pointed at Operator 5 and Tim Donovan, while sharp querying eyes traveled over the natty Purple Empire uniform of Jimmy Christopher and the fur robe and blonde wig of Tim Donovan.

TIM GRINNED, and brought the car to a stop. Now the faces of those dark figures became plainer. They were gaunt, attenuated by hunger and cold and privation. These were lean men, clothed in tatters, and in odds and ends of American Army uniforms. But if they were hungry or cold, their hands, holding the menacing revolvers and knives, were steady enough.

Operator 5 glanced around the circle of faces, and smiled with sympathy. He said in English: "You are expecting me. Where is your commanding officer?"

Some one laughed in the darkness. "Expecting you? Well, maybe not. But you sure stepped into something when you drove down this way! Imagine it, boys—a Purple Empire officer, walking right in on us!"

Jimmy Christopher said: "You're mistaken. I'm not a Purple Empire officer. I'm the man you are expecting—Operator 5."

There was a momentary silence, then: "If you're Operator 5, you'll know the password."

"Paul Revere!" Jimmy Christopher replied promptly.

There was a sigh of astonishment from the men surrounding the car.

"It's Operator 5, all right! Boy! Where'd you get the uniform? And where'd you get the girl?"

"She isn't a girl," Jimmy told them, laughing. "Show them, Tim!"

Tim Donovan grinned, threw off his fur robe, and ripped away the wig. With a rag he rubbed cold-cream from his face, and sat revealed as a pert-nosed, freckle-faced Irish lad of sixteen.

"How do I look, boys?" he demanded gaily.

There were grins, and chuckles of approbation. "Where did you get the uniform and the girl's clothes?"

"From the original owners," Operator 5 told them. "Take a look in the back—under the tarpaulin."

Eagerly the men raised the tarpaulin covering the bulky bundle on the floor in the rear. The figures of a trussed-up man and a girl of fifteen were revealed. They had been in the car all through that wild ride. Effective gags had prevented them from crying out while Operator 5 was being questioned on the bridge.

Jimmy Christopher slid from his seat, went to the rear and very solicitously untied the young girl. She was pretty, blonde-haired, fair-complexioned; and she did not seem to be indignant at the treatment that had been accorded her.

She stepped from the car, threw a shy smile at Operator 5, and proceeded to exercise her arms and legs to restore the circulation. While Jimmy Christopher was untying the bound man in the rear, Tim Donovan approached the girl.

"I'm sorry we had to treat you so rough, miss—"

She shrugged, laughingly. "I do not mind," she said, in a halting sort of English. "Your friend, Operator 5, explained to me carefully why he had to kidnap me, and why it was necessary for me to be tied. He is a gentleman. I do not mind being captured by a gentleman."

Jimmy Christopher untied the man, and the latter climbed out, cursing loudly in the language of the Purple Empire. He glowered at Jimmy.

"You shall die for this, Operator 5! You have committed an unpardonable crime. You have kidnapped the daughter of the Imperial Prime Minister—"

He was close to Operator 5, shaking a fist in his face.

Baron Flexner's daughter called out to him: "Be still, Captain von der Sturm. It is the fortune of war." She smiled. "I am sure no harm will come to me at the hands of Operator 5!"

Jimmy bowed to her. "You can be assured of that, my dear young lady. Our quarters here are poor, but you shall have the best of them. Captain von der Sturm, I apologize deeply for posing as you, but you understand how necessary it was. We would never have been able to enter Philadelphia otherwise."

Von der Sturm still glared. "I can do nothing; I am your prisoner. But one day you shall pay for this impudence. We might even have been shot, lying there, bundled in the bottom of the car, with those machine guns and rifles spitting!"

Tim Donovan broke in. "Not a chance, Captain. The body of that car is bulletproof, and you know it. It's Operator 5 and I who were in danger—with slugs ripping through the canvas top!"

"And now, if you please," Jimmy Christopher said in his most courtly manner, "follow me and I'll get you something to eat."

He turned to the Americans crowding around them. "Where's Frank Ames, your commanding officer?" he asked.

"This way, Operator 5. He didn't come out because he's got a wounded leg—he took a bullet right above the kneecap in that scrap with the Purple Empire troops at the Arkansas River, and he's just recovering from it. But he'll be damned glad to see you. We've been holed up here for a long time now, and we don't know what to do first."

"There'll be plenty to do today!" Jimmy Christopher told them grimly as he conducted Freda Flexner toward the shacks on the river bank.

CHAPTER 2
THE SPARK OF FREEDOM

THE REAL Captain von der Sturm was led away, still protesting volubly, by some of the Americans. They took him to a shack far up in the park, where he would be out of harm's way.

Jimmy Christopher, with Tim Donovan and Freda Flexner, were conducted to another shack, where Frank Ames, their commander, met them.

Frank Ames had been wounded in an almost suicidal undertaking. That maneuver had enabled Operator 5 to capture an important group of Purple Empire ordnance trains, and to gather the nucleus of an army.* Operator 5 had been about to join the American Defense Force on the West Coast, bringing with him the huge guns captured with the ordnance trains, when he learned of the surrender of the American Defense Force. He had been left in command of a secondary, an army without a country, surrounded on every side by the conquering ruthless Purple Empire.

That army, together with the captured ordnance and supplies, he had led into Death Valley, where they were now quartered, ringed around by a bristling wall of steel, consisting of ten crack divisions of Marshal Kremer's shock troops, withdrawn from the Western Front at the cessation of hostilities.

---

* AUTHOR'S NOTE: The story of how Frank Ames virtually thrust himself into the jaws of destruction in order to lure the Purple troops away from the railroad line where the ordnance trains were speeding westward was narrated in the story entitled, "Patriots' Death March." It will be recalled by those who have followed the course of the Purple Invasion that Operator 5 captured those ordnance trains and drove them across half the country, defeating the enemy in two pitched battles, only to learn that the main American Army under Z-7 had been forced to surrender. He then marched his men and supplies into Death Valley. The Americans quartered there numbered almost a hundred thousand, but they dared not make an overt attack against the Purple Empire unless they were assured that the civilian population throughout the country would rise at the same time. Jimmy Christopher's mission at this time was to arrange for this. After the surrender of the American Defense Force, civilians everywhere had become more or less apathetic. Jimmy's task was to arouse them from this apathy.

Jimmy Christopher knew, of course, that Frank Ames had been wounded, but he had not seen him since that fateful day on the bank of the Arkansas River, when he had left the young man to almost certain death, a voluntary sacrifice to his country. Ames' escape  from death had been little short of miraculous, and now these two had much to talk about.

Ames sat up on a cot in a corner of the shack, his back bolstered by a heap of straw. There was nothing resembling a pillow in these crude quarters.

Operator 5, Tim Donovan and Freda Flexner, seated about the wobbly table in the center of the room, ate pork and beans out of tin plates, using pieces of cardboard as spoons.

Frank Ames smiled ruefully at Jimmy Christopher. "I'm sorry, Operator 5, but that's the best I can do in the line of food. We wouldn't have had even that, but some of the boys hijacked a Purple Empire truck yesterday." He grimaced. "All they had on that truck was pork and beans. We'll be eating it for a week!"

One of the men sitting around the room grinned. "At that, Frank it's better than chewing thumbs, the way we had to do before we grabbed this load!"

In the corner of the shack, opposite Frank Ames' cot, was a small pot-bellied stove, upon which one of the men was warming more cans of beans.

"I've got two hundred men here," Ames told Jimmy Christopher. "We've been hiding out for two months in this neck of the woods. Every day a few more men drift in. At night we drill, and we sleep in the day time—just waiting around for a chance to get in a good slam at those Purple polecats. When you radioed that you were coming, we knew there was action in the wind."

Jimmy nodded. "Action is right—if your boys are willing to take a chance in a big way."

Ames glanced at the other men in the room, then grinned at Jimmy Christopher. "Do you need to ask that, Operator 5? But listen—we're all burning up to hear how you grabbed this young lady—and what you intend to do with her." He gestured toward Freda Flexner, who was wolfing pork and beans. She and Tim Donovan were racing to see who could consume the more.

Jimmy shrugged. "It was an accident. Tim and I flew across the country from California, stopping off at a dozen places on the way. We tried to arouse the civilians, to get them to cooperate in a simultaneous rebellion. There's an American army of a hundred thousand men quartered in Death Valley, Frank, and we only need a little cooperation from the rest of the country to come out and give battle to Kremer's divisions."

Ames' eyes were sparkling. "And were the civilians willing—"

Jimmy shook his head. "I'm afraid they're licked, Frank. They have the feeling that it's no use. They don't believe there are that many men in Death Valley, and they say it wouldn't do any good even if there were. The Purple Empire has a strangle-hold on the country now."

Ames grew serious. "What do you plan to do?"

Operator 5's fist clenched on the rude table. "I'm going to

wake them out of their apathy! By God, I'll show them that America is still on the map. I'll *make* them fight!"

Ames leaned forward eagerly, forgetful of his wounded leg.

"How can you do it, Operator 5?"

"By striking blow after blow at the Purple Empire; by striking such telling blows that the civilians will be ashamed to refuse their cooperation. And then, when their spirit is sufficiently aroused, I'll go back to Death Valley and lead that army out against the whole damned Purple Empire! The American civilians won't stand by, idly, when that happens!"

ALL THE men in the room were suddenly tense, imbued with the fiery spirit of Operator 5. It was that spirit which had carried on for ten months in the face of invincible odds; which had placed obstacle after obstacle in the path of the Purple Invasion; which had brought a great armada of airplanes from South America to beat back and destroy a whole fleet of the Purple Empire; which had seized and held a fortress in the heart of the enemy territory; which had brought an ordnance train across the country through the whole might of the Imperial Armies*

---

* Author's Note: These exploits of Operator 5 are familiar to every student of American history. They have been related in previous chronicles of this series. When the Purple Emperor, in the very early days of the Invasion, captured Fort Knox and confiscated our entire store of gold, it was Operator 5 who led a desperate raid, recapturing a good portion of it, and transporting that gold to South America for the purchase of a thousand airplanes. It was with those airplanes that he succeeded in destroying the immense fleet of battleships which were steaming under the emblem of the severed head

and which now, in the face of utter surrender, did not yet admit defeat, but faced the future with the indomitable courage that has brought America through every major crisis in her history!

Jimmy Christopher held these men spellbound as he spoke, outlining his plan. The rain outside was beating down with monotonous insistency upon the miserable roof of the dilapidated, battle-scarred shack. Men drifted in by twos and threes, and stopped, listening eagerly, their hearts beating more swiftly as they realized that they were to be given a chance today to strike—and strike hard—against the ruthless oppressor.

"Ever since the enemy occupied Philadelphia," Jimmy Christopher was saying, "they've been busy at the Hog Island Shipyards. Do you know what they're doing there?"

Frank Ames nodded. "We know. They're building ships. They've put millions of dollars into expanding the yards. Four new battleships are near completion—the biggest the world

and the crossed broadswords to attack San Francisco. And it was Operator 5 who led a small, desperate band into the heart of Pennsylvania, under the very noses of the enemy, to attack and surprise the Purple Empire fortress at Pittsburgh; it was he who then had the courage and the resourcefulness to blow up the mighty Maximilian Dam, thus flooding that entire section of the country and destroying the enemy's huge armament works. These and other exploits of Operator 5 will be remembered as long as America lives. It was by just such daring strokes that he managed to keep at a high level the spirit of an oppressed people; and it was another such attempt that he was about to undertake today, with the aid of these bedraggled Americans on the shores of the Schuylkill River.

has ever seen. They're valued at fifty million American dollars apiece."

"That's right," Jimmy told him. "And they're going to use those battleships in their next campaign—the campaign to conquer South America. Now—" he leaned forward tensely—"what would our people think if they learned that *we had destroyed those four battleships!*"

There were almost fifty of the Americans crowded into the small shack now. And at Jimmy's statement there was a dynamic silence in the room. Then suddenly there was a deep-throated *whoosh* as fifty men expelled their breath in a great sigh.

"You can't do it, Operator 5!" Frank Ames exclaimed. "That's the one place in America where they're not using American forced labor. They've got their own men working on those drydocks, and no American is permitted within two miles of the yards. There's an unbroken cordon of soldiers around the island and the navy yard, and if an American civilian is so much as spotted within sight of the troops, he's shot without question. You couldn't even get within sight of the shipyards, Operator 5. And besides, where would you get the explosives? You'd need a couple of tons—"

Jimmy Christopher gave him a tight smile. "I've figured that out, Frank. As for the explosives, we can get all we want."

"But where—"

"Think, Frank. What's across the river from the shipyards, on the Jersey shore?"

Suddenly Frank Ames snapped his fingers. "My God, why didn't I think of that before! The old DuPont powder works, of

JIMMY   CHRISTOPHER

course! The enemy has been running those plants full blast for months, now!"

But at once, Ames' face lengthened. "Yes, the powder's there—

but how are we going to get it? They've got just as strong a guard at the DuPont plant as at the shipyards—"

"The enemy will give it to us," Jimmy told him cryptically. "They'll give it to us, and they'll help transport it to the yards!"

The men stared at him puzzledly. Frank Ames threw him a queer look, as if to suggest that the strain of the past ten months was finally telling on him.

But Tim Donovan, who had been watching Operator 5 carefully as he spoke, burst out excitedly: "Jimmy! I know how you're going to do it! I bet I know!"

Jimmy waved him to be silent. "I'll tell you the details later. In the meantime, are you boys game to try a stunt that may cost us all our lives?"

"Are we game!" they burst out. "Try us!"

"Can you steal four or five of the enemy's power boats on the river?"

Frank Ames nodded. "Can do, fine! We've been keeping careful track of all the boats on the Schuylkill, figuring we might have use for them one of these days, in case we were discovered here and had to escape. There are three brand new navy tenders, tied up just below Point Breeze with only skeleton crews. We could overpower the crews without a bit of noise."

"Good. Detail fifty men to that job. Do it now, while it's still dark, and while the rain is coming down heavy. Try to capture the crews alive, and preserve their uniforms."

There was no longer any hesitation in Frank Ames' manner as he issued swift orders, naming the men who were to go on the mission. He divided the men into three squads, appointing a leader for each. They were to attack the three tenders simultaneously, at a given signal.

"There won't be more than four or five men aboard each tender—if there's that many," he explained to Operator 5. "The job is in the bag!"

JIMMY WAITED till the men had left. Tim Donovan begged to be allowed to go along with them, but Jimmy would not permit it.

Freda Flexner, who had listened to all this with wide eyes, pouted at Tim Donovan. "You are no gentleman! You have captured me and you must keep me prisoner; you must not leave me!"

Tim Donovan grinned at her. "It's too bad you belong to the enemy, Freda. I'm beginning to like you."

She had been permitted to change back to her own clothes, which Tim Donovan had returned to her, and she looked very pretty, though her dress was a bit crushed and wrinkled.

"You haven't told me yet," Frank Ames said, "how you came to capture the young lady."

Jimmy Christopher's eyes were somber. "As I said before, it was an accident. Tim and I flew in, and landed in a field outside of Camden. We covered the plane as best we could, and started to walk. I was wearing the uniform of a major of engineers, and Tim was dressed as a private. You know, there are a lot of youngsters in Rudolph's armies, recruited from Europe and Asia. Well, we were making out all right, when we were spotted by a Purple patrol, before we got well within the city limits. We didn't know the password, and we had to shoot it out with them. We got three of them, but two escaped. We knew those two would get back to barracks and spread the alarm. Every engineer officer, accompanied by a private, would be stopped. We'd never be able to get into Philadelphia."

"What happened then?" Frank Ames demanded.

Jimmy laughed, threw a friendly glance at Freda Flexner. "Well, Tim and I were holding a council of war, when along came a car, driven by Captain von der Sturm, whom you met. And this young lady was his passenger. They took me for a Purple Empire officer, and von der Sturm informed me that he was driving Baron Flexner's daughter to Philadelphia to be present at some kind of ceremony this morning. Whereupon we proceeded to make them both prisoners. We changed clothing with them, and drove in. The rest I've told you."

"Then," Frank Ames said thoughtfully, "since General von Folda and those guards at the bridge are dead, there is nobody who knows that you are not Captain von der Sturm?"

"That's right."

"And what do you propose to do with Miss Flexner?"

Jimmy's lips tightened. "I'm going to do something that I dislike doing very much—but something that can't be avoided." His eyes met those of Freda Flexner. "I want you to understand that I do not intend to harm you, Freda. But I am going to use you to try to save some one whom I dearly love, from death."

Freda glanced at him trustfully. "I know you wouldn't harm me, Operator 5. You are a gentleman. I was wondering about that. My father, Baron Flexner, keeps telling me always that the Americans are savages, and boil people alive, and eat them. I don't think you are like that."

Tim Donovan burst out laughing. "We used to be like that," he told her, "but we stopped eating the Purple soldiers, because we could never boil them tender enough. We like our meat tender. I bet you would taste good if you were cooked well—"

Jimmy Christopher put a hand over his mouth. "Cut it out, Tim! Don't you see you're scaring her to death?"

Freda Flexner smiled shyly. "I think you are—what do you Americans call it—childing?"

"You mean *kidding!*" Tim gurgled.

Freda's eyes twinkled. "I don't see why my father, and Our Imperial Majesty, hates you so, Operator 5, and you, Tim Donovan. You are both very nice." She grew serious, her childish face expressing concern. "But you were saying, Operator 5, that you wanted to save some one you dearly love—"

Jimmy nodded. "My sister, Nan, and a very good friend, Sergeant MacTavish, are prisoners of the emperor. He intends to execute them, after suitable torture, on the occasion of his coronation as Emperor of America. I'm going to send word to your father that you are my prisoner, and that if Nan is executed, we'll retaliate. You understand? Believe me, Freda, I'll never harm you, but perhaps your father won't think so well of me as you do. He may believe that I'd do the same to you—trying to save my sister."

FREDA FLEXNER'S eyes were round as saucers. "You say—your sister is to be tortured?"

He nodded. "I don't like to tell you this—you're such a sweet

35

child. They've probably kept all these things from you. My sister Nan, and Sergeant MacTavish, are to be crucified four days from today—at your father's orders, by authority of the Emperor."

Frieda Flexner's cheeks grew white as paper. *"Crucified!* Your sister! At my father's orders! I do not believe it!"

For answer, Jimmy Christopher silently drew a folded sheet of paper from his tunic pocket. It was wet and soggy from the rain, and he unfolded it carefully so as not to tear it.

"This was posted," he said laconically, "on the door of the City Hall in Louisville, Kentucky, when we stopped off there, three days ago. I pulled it off."

Slowly, almost reluctantly, Freda Flexner took the poster from him, forced herself to look at it. It was some fifteen inches long, by eight inches in width. It was headed:

PROCLAMATION

and it read as follows:

All Hail to Rudolph I, Emperor of the World!

WHEREAS: The so-called American Defense Force has surrendered to our glorious Imperial Armies, leaving its country without a responsible government—

IT IS DECREED, That all that territory formerly known as the United States shall hereafter be termed THE DOMIN- ION OF NORTH AMERICA, and shall be entered among the names of the Dominions subject to the rule of our glorious Emperor, Rudolph I.

BE IT FURTHER DECREED, That on the 30th day of

May, in this, the Fourth Year of the Purple Empire, there shall be held the ceremony of coronation, whereby Our Imperial Majesty shall assume the duties of Emperor of America. On that day, the persons known as Nan Christopher and Aloysius MacTavish shall be crucified in public opposite the Cathedral of Saint Patrick in the City of New York. Thus does our glorious Emperor repay his enemies!

> Signed,
> Baron Julian Flexner,
> Knight of the Purple Empire,
> Prime Minister Extraordinary To His
> Imperial Majesty,
> Rudolph I.

Frank Ames, Jimmy Christopher and Tim Donovan watched Freda Flexner read that vicious proclamation, while the rain beat incessantly upon the roof and the walls.

At last, she put it down upon the table with a shaking hand.

"I—I must believe it now!" she murmured. "How could my father order a thing like this!"

Tim Donovan put a sympathetic hand over hers. "Don't take it so hard, kid. Maybe he's only obeying orders. It must have been Rudolph's idea to stage the coronation on Memorial Day."

Freda looked up quickly at Operator 5. "I would not blame you if you did the same to me! How you must hate my father! How you must hate me!"

Jimmy smiled at her consideratingly. "Not you, Freda. You're a sweet, warm-hearted child. You're not responsible for the horrors of war, and the passions of ambitious men. But—"

37

"I'll help you save your sister!" she exclaimed. "Bring me pen and paper. I'll write father a letter, so he will have proof that I am your prisoner. I will tell him that you will crucify me, if your sister is executed at the Cathedral. He'll move heaven and earth to stop the executions!"

"Good kid!" Tim Donovan praised. "And I'll carry the message. I want to be sure it gets into the right hands!"

Jimmy Christopher started to shake his head. "Nix, Tim—"

"Nix nothing!" Tim Donovan flung at him. "If you think you're going, you're crazy. You're needed here, and here you'll stay. Frank Ames will keep you here by force if necessary!"

Frank Ames nodded from his cot. "The boy's right, Operator 5. What about your plans for today? You can't walk off like that."

"Besides," Tim urged, "I've got a scheme to get through the enemy lines into New York. And it'll get me an interview with Baron Flexner, too!"

"What's the scheme?" Jimmy demanded.

Tim grinned tantalizingly. "Wouldn't you like to know? I'm not talking till you promise I can go!"

Jimmy Christopher hesitated, looking somberly at the lad. It was bad enough to have Nan in the hands of the Purple Emperor. If he let Tim go, and anything happened to the boy, he would never forgive himself. But the young fellow seemed so eager that he hadn't the heart to refuse.

"All right, Tim, you may go. And may, God protect you!"

CHAPTER 3
TIM TAKES A CHANCE

AS THE morning wore on, wind continued to howl over America, and rain poured down relentlessly in driving sheets. All over the conquered country, Purple troopers kept within their barracks, except for those assigned to patrol and guard duty; and shivering civilians huddled in fireless homes or trod wearily out to their tasks in the forced labor gangs which had been formed in every community.

They tightened their belts around their hungry stomachs, and looked up toward the heavens, allowing the rain to beat upon their faces. The feel of the pure, cold rain was a relief to them from the cramped and squalid misery which had been imposed upon them by the conquerors.

In almost every city, residential districts had been destroyed by bombardment during the invasion. Homes and sleeping quarters were at a premium. As a result, the civilians and their families had been in many cases evicted from their houses and apartments, and bundled into crowded quarters in concentration camps, while the Purple troops and their officers took over the remaining homes.

Men and women were forced to work under the penalty of death; and wherever there was a concentration camp, there could also be found an execution block, with rows of gory heads hung upon a rack—heads of recalcitrant civilians who had demurred at the forced labor draft.

Those heads were a constant reminder to the others that

refusal to work would be punished by
summary execution, not only of the
man himself, but of his entire family.

Men who might ordinarily have
defied the cruel taskmasters of the
Purple Empire blanched at the
thought of seeing their wives and children beheaded. Thus were Americans
throughout the nation forced to bow to the Purple Emperor's
will.

Today they went to their tasks with little hope in their hearts.
They knew that somewhere in southern California there was
still an army of Americans, refusing to surrender, waiting for a
chance to strike at the conqueror; they knew that somewhere,
Operator 5 was working and planning; but they could not bring
themselves to believe that either the Death Valley Army or
Operator 5 could prevail against the now entrenched might of
the Purple Empire.

Perhaps they might have felt differently on that rainy morning if they could have seen the three captured Purple Empire
Navy tenders moving down the Schuylkill River toward the
Hog Island shipyard; or if they could have seen the solitary
plane that battled its way from Philadelphia through wind and
rain toward New York.

Americans and Purple troopers alike, along the route of that
plane, looked up, watched it bucking the terrific headwinds, and
wondered what weighty mission was causing that hardy aviator
to take his life in his hands by going up on such a day.

They would have wondered even more had they known that the ship was piloted by a sixteen-year-old boy. Tim Donovan had learned many things in the few years of his association with Operator 5. His keen young Irish mind picked things up quickly, and without the need of lengthy explanations. And Operator 5 made a good teacher. Jimmy had taught the lad to drive a car, to fly a plane, to handle radio and telegraph instruments. He had shown Tim how to shoot with revolver and rifle, so that the Irish lad could hit a twig rustling in the wind at a hundred yards; he had taught him Morse code, and he had taught him the tricks of hand-to-hand fighting.

Tim Donovan, at sixteen, had become an invaluable assistant to Operator 5. Long before the Purple Invasion, the boy had entertained ambitions of one day being admitted officially to the Intelligence Service of the United States, upon coming of age. Now, there was no longer an Intelligence Service, but Tim Donovan continued to act as Operator 5's unofficial assistant.

STARING GRIMLY into the east, he caught sight of tall silhouettes, the few remaining skyscrapers of Manhattan's once-famous sky-line. Two thirds of those buildings had been destroyed by the great guns of the Purple Empire, but the remaining structures still stood as an eloquent testimonial to the initiative and progressiveness of America.

Tim was flying a three-seater Fallada, one of the very latest type of Purple Empire planes. It was the ship in which he and Operator 5 had flown to Philadelphia. Upon its fuselage remained the severed head and crossed broadswords; and those Purple guards who spotted the ship high up in the air recognized the familiar drone of the Fallada motor knew it for one of their own ships. It had been captured some weeks ago, and kept by Operator 5 for such use.

Tim, passing over Manhattan Island, flew over Queens County, and spotted the familiar terrain around Holmes Airport. This spot had been unused since the invasion, and American scouts had often used it as a secret landing field. Until the secret of its use was discovered by the Purple Empire, it would be safe to continue to land there. But one could never know, until he was actually on the ground, whether the Purple troops were lying in wait to capture the next arrival.

Tim circled twice, scanning the ground below carefully. Fortunately, there was no fog, and visibility was good in spite of the rain. He could see nothing suspicious down there, and at last coming around into the wind, he depressed the stick and came down.

He made a good enough landing, considering the weather, and taxied the plane into the old, dilapidated hangar at the end of the field.

He waited a moment, breathlessly. If the enemy had discovered this field, and were lying in wait, now would be the time for them to rush him. He was ready, with his hand on the swivel-type machine-gun behind his cockpit. But no one showed.

At last, convinced that his landing had been unobserved, he climbed out of the cockpit, dragging a small bundle after him.

His problem now was to get across one of the bridges into Manhattan. He was about to put to the test the plan about which he had spoken to Operator 5 in Philadelphia.

The rain pattered on the metal sides and roof of the hangar, while the boy swiftly peeled off his flying togs, and then took off his outer clothing. Next, he opened the bundle, extracted from it a torn, dirty coat, torn at the shoulder, and patched in a half dozen places. There was also a pair of trousers, one leg of which was almost entirely gone from the knee down. He put on these two dilapidated garments, making a wry face of disgust as he did so.

He went outside into the rain and scooped up handfuls of wet, soggy earth, smeared it on his face, and on the exposed parts of his legs where they showed through the torn trousers. Then, returning into the hangar, he took from the bundle a long, bright scarlet sash, and a leather belt with a small holster attached. In the holster rested a thirty-two automatic, and there were six pockets around the belt that accommodated six extra clips of ammunition.

He tied the trousers around with a piece of rope, which he knotted in front, allowing the ends to hang down. Then, he tied the sash around his waist and up across his left shoulder, much in the fashion of a Sam Browne belt.

Standing erect now, he looked down at himself, surveying his disreputable appearance. He looked like an urchin that hadn't been washed for a year. From the almost empty bundle at his feet he now took a small make-up kit, and applied a paste-like substance to his face, around the eyes and mouth, and down along his throat. The paste-like substance, mingling with the mud he had already put on, gave him the appearance of being almost entirely covered with revolting sores.

ADMIRAL
COUNT
VON
UHL

FREDA
FLEXNER

BARON
FLEXNER

At last he was ready to leave. He carefully closed the hangar doors, and started off across the field, toward Manhattan. He came out onto the road, his heart beating a little rapidly. The rain beat down upon him, sending the caked earth trickling down his body in little rivulets of mud.

He shuddered. "Gosh," he murmured aloud, "I hope I look as terrible as I feel!"

Those sores and that scarlet sash marked him for one of that great army of unfortunates who had filtered into America with the Purple Invasion—the army of lepers!

Rudolph's conquests had extended over eastern Europe, India, Turkestan, Arabia, and all of Asia. Thousand of lepers lived in the many countries under the rule of the Purple Emperor, and the disease had spread widely in the last four years. This age-old disease, at one time almost conquered by the humanitarian advances of modern civilization, had found for itself a gruesome recrudescence under the careless rule of Rudolph.

For the Purple Emperor had no time for medical care of the millions of people now under his dominion. Every resource of science and medicine was turned toward the goal of devising newer and more terrible methods of making war. Life was the cheapest thing in the vast Purple Empire—and if millions died of disease, then other millions were endlessly being spawned in the slums of Europe and Asia—millions who were destined to carry arms for the greater glory of their emperor, conqueror of half the world.

So it was not strange that leprosy spread at an even greater pace than during the Middle Ages. So numerous had the lepers become that Emperor Rudolph was at last constrained to issue an edict concerning them. That edict was not drafted for the purpose of ameliorating the condition of the sufferers, but merely to protect the armed troops. All lepers were compelled to wear a distinctive sash, of vivid scarlet color, so that men of the Purple Empire could keep their distance from them.

And these pitiable figures were to be seen in the streets of almost every occupied city in America. Ostracized by all, these poor men and women could do nothing to earn a living except to beg at corners for a crust of bread with which to sustain life.

It was as a leper that Tim Donovan planned to enter New York and make his way about without being stopped or questioned!

THE WALK into town was a long, wet and dreary one. Dozens of military cars passed him, but none stopped to offer him a lift. At the bridge, the guard motioned him impatiently to pass, and shouted: "Keep your distance, leper. Step nearer, and I will shoot you like a dog!"

Tim Donovan lowered his head and stepped out on the long bridge over the East River. At the Manhattan side he was also permitted to pass; and he drew a long breath of relief when he found himself at last on Manhattan Island.

New York City, he saw, was different from the New York of a year before. Gone were the gay crowds and the bustling noise of Broadway. Now, civilians with bowed heads scuttled through the streets, trying desperately to avoid the strutting Purple Empire officers. Purple troopers were everywhere, and patrols stopped men and women, demanding to see their passes. All civilians

were given an identification card by the
Governor of the Occupied Territory.
That card was stamped each day by the
commander of the Forced Labor Division to which they belonged. If a civilian was stopped and found to have a
card that was not properly stamped, he
was arrested, and executed within two hours.

So numerous had become the executions of late that the
official headsman could not keep up with the demand for
his services. As a result, Rudolph had installed a guillotine in
Central Park. The bloody instrument was in operation when
Tim Donovan passed by. In the mall, where free American citizens had once come to listen to concerts, those same Americans
were being herded in tumbrils, their last ride.

Tim, watching from Fifth Avenue, felt his blood boil as he
saw one after another being led up the three short steps of the
execution platform, to kneel in the rain and bow their heads
over the block. Then a swift descent of the glistening blade, and
another head fell into the basket. The executioner would grin,
lift the head up so that the troops could see it. There would be a
cheer from the Purple troopers, the head would drop back into
the basket, and the next victim would be led up.

Tim Donovan waited while five heads fell in quick succession. Then, with a feeling of nausea at the pit of his stomach,
he turned away, hastened up Fifth Avenue. He passed close to
a patrol of Purple Empire troopers, and they shooed him away
with the points of their bayonets.

Tim had picked up enough of the language of the Purple Empire to be able to talk it passably well. There were so many nationalities represented among the subjects of Rudolph that a little accent was not regarded as strange. So Tim called out to the patrol:

"A little alms, please. In the name of our glorious Emperor, give a little alms to a starving leper!"

The troopers guffawed. One of them said: "Here, you leper—catch this. If you're hungry enough, you can eat it!"

The man threw something, and Tim caught it, stood there holding it, while the patrol passed on, laughing uproariously. Tim felt a sudden flood of rage, felt his cheeks burning under the mud and make-up on his face. The thing that the trooper had thrown him was the severed finger of a child! The small, pitiful object, still fresh and bloody, burned the palm of Tim's hand. It told its own story of cruelty and torture. With a sudden agonized cry, Tim Donovan flung the severed finger from him. The troopers had passed down the street, and did not even look back.

Tim, with tears at the corners of his eyes, continued on his way. Pictures flooded his mind. Behind him, on the mall, men and women were losing their heads to satisfy the cruel hate of a blood-lusting emperor. Somewhere, a child lay without a finger—and God knew what else had been done to it—while its mother lay in another room, dead perhaps, and fortunate if death had come to her quickly. For the Purple troopers were encouraged by their commanders to commit torture and rape upon the defenseless civilians.

Poignantly, Tim Donovan cataloged in his memory the face

of the trooper who had thrown him the severed finger, storing up each coarse feature, in his mind's eye. Some time, perhaps, he would meet that trooper again, under different circumstances; and then he would be sure to avenge that pitiful child.

TIM SHUFFLED north, his feet sloshing on the rain-soaked ground. The pavement was torn up in many places, scarred by shells that had exploded here during the bombardment of New York in the early days of the invasion. All along the way, gangs of civilians in the Forced Labor Details were working, repairing the streets, laying new pavements, repairing damaged buildings. And always they were under the eagle scrutiny of guards with ready rifles.

He dared not walk too fast, lest he excite suspicion. Other men with scarlet sashes were on the streets, begging, but none of the lepers walked fast. These men had nowhere to go, and they never hurried. It was almost evening before the lad reached his objective—the tall bluff on upper Riverside Drive where Rudolph had erected his great palace—where Baron Julian Flexner would be; Baron Flexner, whose daughter was now a captive of Operator 5 in Philadelphia—the same Baron Flexner who had ordered the crucifixion of Nan Christopher and Sergeant MacTavish. Tim knew too, that somewhere in that huge building there were cells; and that Nan and the sergeant were confined there.

He was weary from his long walk, and he squatted on the ground close to the bank of the Hudson River, staring up at the tall cliff and the palace at its top. He had entered New York. He had Frieda Flexner's letter in his pocket. Now he must find some means of meeting Flexner, of giving him that letter.

The boy was soaked, wet, cold and shivering. He had eaten nothing since leaving Philadelphia that morning, but he could not have eaten at that particular moment even if the most appetizing dishes had been set before him. From up there in the palace, a myriad lights shone, and the noise and shouts of unrestrained gaiety drifted down. There was some sort of ball going on up there.

And while these conquerors danced and sang, Tim reflected bitterly, an American army was bottled up in Death Valley, three thousand miles away; men and women were being beheaded in Central Park; women and children were being mutilated in hundreds of cities throughout the land; and Operator 5 must be working somewhere toward his ultimate goal of arousing the nation to victorious rebellion.

At that last thought, Tim Donovan felt a sudden surge of anxiety. When he had left Philadelphia, the captured Navy tenders of the Purple Empire had been anchored in the Schuylkill River, ready to set forth for the attempt upon Hog Island. Had Jimmy Christopher been successful in that undertaking, or had the odds against him been too great? Had he struck a tremendous blow at the power and the prestige of the Purple Empire, or did his dead body even now float down the Delaware River with the bodies of Frank Ames and those other Americans who had volunteered to accompany him on the mad venture?

Tim Donovan suddenly felt very young, and very much alone,

and very wet and cold. He bit his lower lip to keep it from trembling, felt of the automatic holstered under his waistband, and started resolutely to climb the cliff toward the palace above.

CHAPTER 4
FIFTY AGAINST A FLEET

WHILE TIM DONOVAN had been jockeying down to a landing in the airport outside New York City that morning, Philadelphia was just coming to life for the day.

Bugles sounded in the barracks of the Purple Empire, and Purple troopers hastened out to relieve the night watch. Weary, cowed civilians were herded out of concentration camps to resume their back-breaking labors for another day.

In the shipyards in South Philadelphia, day was no different from night. Twenty-four hours a day the engineer corps of the Purple Empire labored at the task of completing the four giant battleships that were to be used in the campaign against South America. All around those shipyards a ring of guards kept everyone at a distance, while in the Delaware River the battleship *Kondor* stood guard over the river approach to the yards.

The *Kondor* was the flagship of Admiral Count Anton von Uhl, who was to command the expedition to South America. It was under his personal supervision that those four ships were being constructed.

All along both shores of the Delaware the hum of manufacturing activity had continued through the night, and went on without interruption except for change of laboring shifts. The huge DuPont Works on the Jersey side of the Delaware were turning out a ton per minute of *Electro-thermite No. 3*, the new, high-powered explosive devised by the Purple Empire. This was the most powerful explosive yet invented by man. Its use in a 155 mm shell increased the effective destruction-radius of the shell by two hundred percent. A pound and a half of *Electro-thermite No. 3*, detonated by a radio impulse, could destroy everything within a radius of two hundred feet, and could rip apart the armor-plate of a battleship as easily as it could tear the arms of a man from their sockets.

The four new battleships now being built would be the first to have guns equipped to fire *Electro-thermite No. 3* shells. Even the smaller anti-aircraft guns would use the new explosive; and Purple Empire engineers calculated that a barrage of *Electro-thermite* from anti-aircraft guns mounted on a ship would bring down every plane in the air within a radius of a thousand feet, by the mere force of concussion.

Altogether, Admiral Count von Uhl was very well pleased with the way things were going as he sipped his early morning coffee on the bridge of the battleship *Kondor* that rainy morning.

His aide and personal adjutant, Naval Lieutenant Hjalmar Beyn, stood respectfully at his elbow, reading dispatches from the various units of the Imperial Navy, which were cruising up and down the Atlantic Seaboard.

The Admiral was large, fat and heavy. His beefy face was fixed in contemplation while Lieutenant Beyn's rasping voice read one dispatch after another. But Admiral Count von Uhl was listening with only half an ear. His eyes were following in puzzlement

the three small navy tenders which had
appeared from the Schuylkill River, and
were chugging out past the Navy Yard
into the Delaware.

Von Uhl leaned forward in his seat,
putting down his coffee cup, and raised
his hand, motioned Lieutenant Beyn to
silence. Beyn stopped reading.

Von Uhl frowned. "What are those
tenders doing?" he demanded. "Why are
they here? I issued no orders for them
to move!"

Beyn shook his head. "I do not
understand, sir. The tenders were to remain in the Schuylkill
River until further orders—"

Von Uhl picked up his field glasses, focused them upon the
leading tender.

"That is strange," he murmured. "The commander of that
first boat seems to be an Imperial Intelligence officer. I did not
know—"his voice suddenly snapped—"Here, Beyn! Have a boat
put over the side, and go to meet those tenders. Find out what
they are doing here!"

"Perhaps I should semaphore them, sir? They seem to be
heading directly across the river, toward the powder works."

"Very good, Beyn. Do so at once!" Beyn saluted, and
summoned the signalman from the chart house. In a moment
the man had his semaphores wagging.

"What are you doing here?" he signaled at Beyn's direction. *"Who is in command of your boats?"*

ADMIRAL COUNT VON UHL picked up his glasses once more, focused them on the leading tender. He saw that the officer in charge, with the assistance of a subaltern, was decoding the message, while a seaman was breaking out the semaphore signals from the lockers.

Almost at once the officer in charge of the tender, whom von Uhl had identified as an Imperial Intelligence Captain, took the semaphores from the seaman, and proceeded to reply.

"Respects to Admiral Count von Uhl, from Captain Hugo von der Sturm, of Imperial Intelligence. Have taken over command of tenders by special order of His Imperial Majesty. Will report to Admiral Count von Uhl in person within fifteen minutes."

Von Uhl frowned in vexation. "He is insolent, that captain!" The Admiral rose wrathfully from his chair. "Imperial order or not, he must report to me at once. Fifteen minutes!" Von Uhl snorted. "Am I a nobody? Beyn! Semaphore him to come aboard at once and explain his insolence—"

"Pardon, sir," Beyn expostulated. "Would that be wise? If this captain should turn out to be some court favorite of the emperor's—"

"Humph!" Von Uhl grunted. "Perhaps you are right. I seem to have heard of a Captain von der Sturm. He is an aide of Baron Flexner's—assigned to accompany the Baron's daughter. Well, let us wait and see what he does."

Lieutenant Beyn motioned to the signalman to retire, and the two officers watched the tenders move across the river toward the powder plant. Beyn appeared puzzled. "He seems to have a large complement of men on board those three boats, sir—more than the regular crews of the tenders. Do you suppose he has brought some of his own men?"

"Who knows? He may be carrying out special instructions relative to the launching of the four battleships."

They watched the tenders pull in to the dock at the opposite shore, saw the Intelligence Captain being met there by an officer in charge of the powder plant, and saw the captain present a letter of some sort.

At once the officer in charge of the powder plant saluted. There was a little wait, while von Uhl and Beyn peered through their glasses impatiently. Then they saw wheelbarrows being trundled down to the dock, loaded with small black packing cases, which were transferred to the three tenders.

Von Uhl was puzzled. "Those are cases of *Electro-thermite No. 3!*" he told Beyn. What can he want with them?"

"He is also loading a radio-impulse detonator on board his tender," Beyn supplemented. "Strange, sir—"

The tenders cast off from the dock, and chugged back across the river toward the shipyards, where the completed hulls of the four great battleships loomed in the gloomy rain, on their immense drydocks.

At the drydock, the tenders began to unload their cases of explosive, and the Admiral could see that the shipyard workers were aiding the crews of the tenders to carry those cases on board the battleships.

While this was going on, the Intelligence Captain returned

aboard his tender and cast off, heading toward the *Kondor*, and leaving the other two tenders and their crews to complete whatever curious task they were engaged in.

"Here he comes," von Uhl growled. "The man must have Imperial orders, since the officers at the powder plant and the shipyard all seemed eager to obey his commands."

The tender pulled up alongside the *Kondor*, and a ladder was lowered. The Intelligence Captain, followed by the entire crew of his tender, came aboard. Two of the tender crew carried up the radio-impulse detonator, which they had acquired at the powder plant.

THERE WERE almost fifty men in the party from the tender, and they were all armed, some of them with sub-machine guns. Many of them wore the uniforms of seamen in the Navy of the Purple Empire, but many others were clad only in dirty dungarees.

Jimmy Christopher, still attired in his natty Intelligence Department uniform, swaggered insolently across the deck toward the bridge, while his men swarmed up the ladder behind him. He had used all the available uniforms of the captured Purple Empire seamen on the three tenders, dressing as many of Ames' men as he could in them. The Americans who manned the other two tenders were attired in extra dungarees which they had found in the lockers of the tenders.

Now, as Jimmy approached the bridge, Admiral Count von Uhl stepped to the rail, exclaimed cholerically: "Here, here! What's this! Why are you bringing all your men aboard? By what right—"

Jimmy had already climbed the companion, followed by Frank Ames and the two men who carried the detonator. He saluted the admiral with an affectation of carelessness, and withdrew a folded document from his tunic pocket.

"Orders from His Imperial Majesty to Admiral Count von Uhl!" he said.

Von Uhl glowered at him. He intended to cook this insolent captain's hash at the first opportunity. But first he wanted to see what was in those orders.

He unfolded the document under Jimmy's cool glance, and his face reddened as he read. At the top of the sheet was the engraved facsimile of the severed head and the crossed broadswords that appeared on all Imperial Communications. Beneath it, written in the fine script of the Purple Empire, were several lines of writing, followed by the signature of Rudolph I, himself.

Von Uhl restrained his anger as he read the orders. He did not know that this document had been cleverly forged by Jimmy Christopher. He did not notice that the engraved heading was carefully pasted to the sheet of writing paper. That heading had come off the printed proclamation which Jimmy Christopher had shown to Freda Flexner. He had cut it off, pasted it on a fresh sheet of paper, and then written in his order below it, imitating the signature of Rudolph from the printed facsimile on various proclamations which had been posted in public from time to time.

Jimmy Christopher had spent almost two hours in the writing of that document, and he was proud of the job. He watched von Uhl's face as the Admiral read it:

Imperial Headquarters
of the
Armies of Occupation
of the
Central Empire

To All Officers of the Army, Navy & Air Force,

Greeting:

The bearer of these presents, Hugo von der Sturm, Captain of Imperial Intelligence, is hereby vested with Extraordinary Authority for the purpose of carrying out a special mission assigned to him. Upon his demand, all officers of the Armies of Occupation, as well as officers of the Navy and Air Force, shall carry out his orders without question as if those orders were issued directly from Imperial Headquarters. Captain von der Sturm's mission is important and of the utmost secrecy, and no questions of any kind shall be asked.

Signed,

Rudolph, R.I.

VON UHL finished reading, and handed back the paper, reluctantly. "It seems," he growled, "that I have no alternative but to obey your orders. What do you wish, Captain von der Sturm?"

Jimmy Christopher bowed in his best Central Empire manner, while behind him, Frank Ames and the two Americans who had carried up the detonator breathed deep sighs of relief. They had felt acute misgivings as to how the Admiral would receive the strange order.

"If you will permit us," Jimmy said suavely, "my men will hook

Operator 5 leaped to the detonator, pushed down the plunger!

this detonator up to your radio equipment. We are conducting an experiment of vital importance to the Empire."

Von Uhl shrugged, motioned to Lieutenant Beyn. "Show them the radio room, Beyn." He led Beyn to one side. "What do you think, Beyn?" he asked in a whisper. "This thing sounds peculiar to me."

Beyn nodded. "It is peculiar, sir. But then, Imperial Head-quarters often does peculiar things. One does not dare to question such an order—"

"Naturally," von Uhl rasped. "But one can check up on it. Is our ship-to-shore telephone still hooked up?"

"Yes, sir."

"Then, as soon as you have shown these men to the radio room, phone to Imperial Headquarters in New York, and verify the order. They can have no objection to our doing that!"

Beyn saluted. "Very good, sir."

The Purple Empire lieutenant led the two Americans away toward the radio room. Those two men had been carefully picked from Frank Ames' forces. They were experts in radio. As they followed Beyn, one of them unwound a long coil of wire from a large spool. The loose end of the wire was already connected to the detonator. The other end would be hooked up to the radio sending equipment.

Jimmy Christopher stepped to the detonator, stood there in an attitude of bored patience. Von Uhl paced up and down the bridge, occasionally throwing a vicious glance in Jimmy's direction. He did not relish thus being superseded in command on his own bridge, even by Imperial order.

Frank Ames leaned over the rail, watching the deck below. All the Americans had already come up on deck, and they were lined up in double column. One of them had a small case of *electro-thermite*, to which he was connecting a six-volt battery. Frank Ames watched the man finish his work. That battery had come from the powder plant across the river. It was used for detonating test shots of explosive in concrete explosion-test rooms. Now it was to be used for a far different purpose.

The man on the deck below arose from his task, raised his hand in signal to Frank Ames. Quickly Ames waved back, then walked over to Jimmy Christopher.

"All set on the deck below, Operator 5," he reported. Then he added: "I'm nervous as hell about this, Operator 5. So far, everything is going smoothly; but a thousand things can happen. Don't forget that there are twelve hundred men on this ship, and we've only got fifty. They could wipe us out—"

Jimmy Christopher smiled. "They could, but I don't think they will. You see, the difference is that they don't want to die, while our men are ready to give up their lives. When you're not afraid to die, Frank, you have a great advantage over the enemy!"

Ames nodded. "You're right about that, Operator 5. But this is the most reckless stunt I've ever heard of—blowing up the enemy's ships, with the enemy's own explosive, and using the enemy's own equipment to do it! If it succeeds, we'll go down in history, Operator 5—and if it fails, we'll all go up in little pieces!"

They were interrupted by the return of the two Americans from the radio room. One of them saluted Jimmy Christopher. "We are ready, *Herr* Captain," he reported, speaking in the language of the Purple Empire for the benefit of von Uhl. Then he came closer, whispered in English: "The detonator is connected, Operator 5. We've set the radio beam on the agreed wave length. If the boys on the other tenders have set their receiving equipment properly, there shouldn't be any hitch!"

Jimmy nodded. "I'm watching for their signal. Any trouble, Johnson?"

Johnson grinned. "The operator in the radio room got suspicious. He heard me and Fields talking in English, and he tried to sneak out. We had to bop him one. We tied him up, and we locked the radio room, so nobody can get in to tamper with our adjustments."

Jimmy nodded his approval. "Good boys." He swung around, fixed his eyes on the shipyards, where the four large hulks of the nearly completed battleships loomed through the rain.

THE MEN on the deck below were quiet, tense, waiting for the signal from shore. Jimmy Christopher had made his plans as airtight as possible, but there were many possibilities of a slip. Those men on the other two tenders had been entrusted with a task fully as difficult as this one on the *Kondor*. It was their job to set up a load of *electro-thermite* in each of the four ships in dry dock, and to hook the explosive up with a radio receiving set. Any false move they might make would ruin the entire plan.

Now, as Jimmy Christopher kept his eyes on the shore, Admiral von Uhl came up behind him. "May I ask, Captain, how long you intend to remain on board?" His voice was silkily restrained. "Perhaps I can have some tea served—"

Jimmy was not listening. He had just seen the two tenders put out from the shipyard, and almost at once, a Very pistol from the leading tender sent its colored flare up into the sky.

That was the signal!

Jimmy stepped toward the detonator. If all the connections had been properly made, the down-stroke of that detonator would be heard around the world!

CHAPTER 5
A BLAST TO WAKE A NATION

THE DESTRUCTION of these four battleships, though in itself not a mortal blow to the Purple Empire, would be of vital importance to America. Such a brilliantly daring *coup* would stir the civilian residents of the country deeply, would perhaps serve to awaken in them the spark of resistance which had died down under the murk of oppression.

It would show Americans everywhere that there was still hope for liberty; and it might cause thousands—perhaps millions—to flock to the banner of the American Army in Death Valley. That was what Operator 5 wanted more than anything else. And he was risking his own life and the life of all the other men under Ames' command, to attain that goal.

So he could not be blamed if his heart beat just a little faster as he stepped toward the detonator. The next instant might well be the one that would decide the fate of America.

And it was just then that Lieutenant Beyn came rushing out of the chart room, and shouting: "Stop him! Stop him! He is an impostor! Imperial Headquarters issued no such orders!"

Von Uhl had been waiting for Beyn to return from the ship-to-shore telephone. His face lit up with ugly triumph, and he whipped out his sword, rushed headlong at Operator 5. Beyn erupted on to the bridge, sword in hand also, while behind him, half a dozen seamen of the Purple Empire came running, armed with pistols.

Jimmy Christopher was still several paces from the detonator. Von Uhl's attack would cut him off from that handle. It was a moment such as this which he had dreaded, hoping that he would be given enough grace before being discovered, to set off the charge of *electro-thermite*. Apparently that was not to be accomplished without a fight.

His own sword hung in the scabbard at his side. He drew it, swinging to meet von Uhl's mad rush, and the two blades clashed with flashing sparks. In the meantime, Frank Ames had also drawn his sword, and engaged Lieutenant Beyn, while Johnson and Fields drew guns and began to fire steadily and methodically at the seamen rushing from the chart room.

Down on deck a petty officer blew a whistle, and Central Empire marines came running from their quarters to attack the Americans on the deck. In a second the quietness of the ship was transformed into a maelstrom of furious fighting.

JIMMY CHRISTOPHER skillfully parried von Uhl's thrusts, trying at the same time to maneuver the Admiral away from the detonator. Von Uhl guessed his purpose, and attacked with redoubled fury. The man was no mean swordsman, and Jimmy Christopher recognized that he would not be able to dispose of him easily.

Revolvers were barking all around, as Johnson and Fields exchanged volleys with the enemy seamen. Frank Ames fought desperately with Beyn, sweat pouring down his face. Beyn was the better swordsman of the two, and Ames realized that the other would run him through within a very few minutes.

The Americans on the deck below were hopelessly outnumbered. In a short time they would be wiped out. If Jimmy Christopher did not succeed in setting off the detonator at once, the chance would be lost forever.

Fiercely, Jimmy lunged, disdaining to parry von Uhl's cunning thrust. The Admiral's sword point touched Jimmy Christopher's throat, pricking the skin; but Jimmy's own weapon, leaping out like a live thing, sped accurately toward the admiral's left eye. Von Uhl might have held his ground, thrust his sword through Jimmy's throat; but the sight of Operator 5's gleaming blade darting at his eye unnerved him. He stepped quickly back, drawing his sword point away from Jimmy's throat.

And in that instant of respite, Operator 5 leaped across to the detonator, pushed down the plunger!

Von Uhl must have realized the purpose of the detonator. He uttered a choked cry, sprang forward. But he was too late.

A rolling barrage of thunder seemed suddenly to have been unleashed upon the world. Geyser-like cascades of plumed smoke and flaming spars erupted from the four battleships in the drydocks. The three tender-loads of *electro-thermite* concentrated in those four ships drove through the steel reinforced armor plate of the great ships as if those plates had been made of butter. The great steel frames burst asunder, and the bulking shapes of the battleships collapsed like a house of cards.

Under the very eyes of those on the *Kondor*, two hundred millions worth of floating fortresses were destroyed.

The terrific force of the explosions rocked the *Kondor*, sending men staggering pell-mell, without regard to friend or foe. The two little tenders out on the river slewed perilously, and seemed to right themselves only by a great effort; then, instead of turning to flee, they headed directly for the *Kondor!*

Von Uhl, staggering against the rail where the repercussion of the explosions had flung him, screamed: *"Himmel!* He has destroyed the ships! Under our noses! *Get that man!"*

He was barely able to make his voice heard, for there were repeated detonations from the drydock, as other cases of *electro-thermite* exploded, one after the other. Jimmy Christopher's men had worked well at the drydock. They had laid a powder train to a long line of *electro-thermite* cases, and these went, one after the other.

Admiral von Uhl steadied himself on the rocking bridge, preparing to lunge at Jimmy Christopher, while Frank Ames and Lieutenant Beyn fenced precariously, barely maintaining their balance. Johnson and Field were on their knees, revolvers raised, covering the entrance to the chart house, from which other Purple Empire officers were swarming.

Down below on the deck, the Purple marines were attacking the fifty men from the tender, while a sub-machine gun somewhere aft began to chatter. It would be only a matter of moments before the gallant raiding party would be completely wiped out.

But Operator 5 still had one ace in the hole. He blew a shrill blast on a whistle he had drawn from his pocket, and the combatants involuntarily ceased fighting, stared up to where he stood. Von Uhl, about to charge him, paused uncertainly, and the machine gun became silent.

Jimmy Christopher took advantage of the lull. He stepped to the bridge rail, pointed dramatically down at the American on the deck below, who knelt beside the case of *electro-thermite*. A dozen other Americans had formed a protective circle about this man, so that the attacking marines could not get at him. And thus guarded, he held two strands of wire, one in each hand.

Those wires ran from the six-volt battery to the case of explosive, and it was apparent to everyone that when he joined the two naked ends of the wire the circuit would be completed.

A deep sigh went up from the Purple Empire marines, and from the officers on the bridge. Death was staring them in the face.

JIMMY CRIED out in the language of the Purple Empire: "When I give the word, that circuit will be closed. There is enough *electro-thermite* in that case to blow you all to hell. I give you one minute to throw down your arms and surrender!"

He turned and stared grimly up at the huge electric clock above the bridge, as if to time his ultimatum. "Touch those wires when I whistle, Blaine!" he ordered the man at the battery.

The men on deck stood in quivering uncertainty, their eyes fixed fascinatedly on the two bare ends of wire in Blaine's hands.

"It's a bluff!" von Uhl screamed to his marines. If the *elec-*

tro-thermite explodes, they will die too! Attack, men! Wipe them out!"

And he leaped at Operator 5, thrusting with his sword.

Jimmy Christopher faced him grimly, deftly flipped his wrist, catching von Uhl's blade close to the hilt. The sword flew out of the Admiral's hand, and von Uhl stood disarmed, panting with hate, glaring at Operator 5.

Jimmy now swung swiftly toward the deck. "Yes," he shouted, "we will all die if that case explodes. But we Americans are ready to die. We gave up our lives for lost when we undertook this task. We are all living on borrowed time, and if you do not surrender, we will set off the *electro-thermite*, and pay our debt to fate!"

He leaned over, while Ames held Lieutenant Beyn at bay with his sword. "If you think we're bluffing," he shouted tensely, "now is the time to attack. *There are only four seconds left!*"

He placed the whistle to his lips, preparatory to blowing it, and Blaine moved the two ends of the wire closer.

Von Uhl shouted: "No, no! Don't believe him—"

But the Admiral was too late. Spurred by the swiftly moving hand of the clock, the marines began to throw down their rifles with desperate haste, hoping to forestall the explosion. *They believed that the Americans were ready to die!*

Von Uhl was weeping tears of rage as his men surrendered on the deck below. Jimmy Christopher breathed a deep sigh of relief, and exchanged glances with Frank Ames.

"That was close, boy!" he grinned. He swung to von Uhl, Beyn, and the other officers on the bridge. "I suggest that you gentlemen surrender also. You can do nothing without your crew's support. What do you say, Admiral Count von Uhl?" he demanded sharply.

Von Uhl bowed his head. "The—ship is—yours!" he said huskily.

Jimmy Christopher smiled. "You have saved the lives of all of us, Admiral!"

He waited on the bridge, while Frank Ames hurried below to the deck, and supervised the taking over of the ship by the Americans. In twenty minutes, the Purple Empire flag had been pulled down, replaced by the Stars and Stripes. The Americans from the two tenders swarmed aboard, and were assigned to positions of command.

Von Uhl and the other officers were placed in detention, but the greater number of the crew remained at their posts, supervised by armed Americans. They took the change cheerfully. Many of them welcomed the relief from the stern discipline of the Purple Navy.

And now, with thousands of men and women lined up along the shore to watch in wonder, the former Purple Empire first-line battleship *Kondor*, flagship of the Imperial Navy, steamed down the Delaware River under the American flag!

THROUGHOUT THE barracks of the enemy in Philadelphia, the alarm spread. Troops were turned out, rushed down to the shore. But their rifle and machine-gun fire was ineffectual against the armor plate of the *Kondor*. The great flagship of the Imperial Navy steamed down the Delaware like a huge mastodon, ignoring the flea bites of lesser animals.

And then, as she passed Chester Island, her own long eighteen-inch guns flamed into action. Operator 5 had set the sights of those guns himself.

Shell after shell erupted from their massive maws, speeding with destructive accuracy toward the DuPont Powder Plant on the Jersey side of the Delaware River. The *Kondor* was shelling the powder plant!

And now, mingling with the deep-throated detonations of the heavy naval guns, there came the rumbling of explosion after explosion from the powder plant. If the destruction of the four battleships in the drydock had been ten times as devastating, it would yet have paled beside the holocaust that now struck the enemy. Here, in the Powder Plant, were massed the concentrated explosives that had been destined for the shells of every gun in every great ship of the Imperial Navy—*electro-thermite* in quantities such as had never been gathered in one place before.

As storehouse after storehouse was struck, the sky was literally rent asunder by the violence of the expanding explosives. The waters of the Delaware were churned as if the earth itself were rocking in an overwhelming upheaval. Flames spread with terrifying rapidity, and the Purple Empire troops gave over all attempts at retaliating upon the *Kondor*, in their desperate efforts to save themselves from the racing fires.

This was indeed a major blow at the very sinews of the Purple Empire.

On the bridge of the *Kondor* as she steamed down toward the open sea, Operator 5 stood gazing backward with somber eyes. All the Americans were silent, refraining from expressions of joy at this unexpected triumph.

The guns had ceased firing. Jimmy Christopher spoke into the deck-telegraph: "Tell the gun-crews they did a fine job!"

Then he straightened, turned to Frank Ames. "Maybe this will wake the country up!" he exclaimed.

Ames' eyes were shining. "And how! We've got to get this news around."

Jimmy nodded. "We'll broadcast on the ship's short wave set. The amateur radios throughout the country will pick it up, and spread the good word."

Freda Flexner, who had been on the second tender, dressed in dungarees like the men, came up to the bridge. Her youthful face was troubled. "My father will be very angry about this," she said.

Jimmy and Ames both laughed at her innocent seriousness.

"Don't worry, Freda," Jimmy told her, patting her on the back. "Your father won't blame you."

"I'm not thinking about myself," she replied. "I was thinking about your little friend, Tim Donovan. He must be in New York now. Perhaps he has already given my letter to my father. And father may grow very angry at this news, and have him executed. I—I would be very sorry if that happened."

Operator 5's eyes were sober. "I wonder how Tim is making out," he murmured. "If that kid gets himself crucified, I'd never be able to live with myself!"

"Me, too!" Freda Flexner said in perfectly idiomatic English.

"It's up to Tim now," Ames said. "There's nothing we can do for him, till he gets away from New York. Can we meet him?"

Jimmy nodded. "We'll stand off the Jersey coast, the way we

agreed with him. We'll give him two days, then if he doesn't turn up, we sail."

Freda Flexner's eyes opened wide. "You'd leave him there?"

"Yes, Freda. We've got other things to do. This isn't a personal war. I love Tim, and I love my sister Nan. But the country is fighting for its life. The next week may be the turning point. The future liberty of America depends on how fast we act now that we've struck a hard blow. And no personal considerations must be allowed to interfere."

Operator 5's face was grim, hard. "If Tim isn't there, we've got to go without him." It was evident that every word he was saying was tearing at his heart. He gulped, went on. "But why think about that? We'll hope he makes it, and meets us—with Nan and Sergeant MacTavish."

"And then what?" Frank Ames asked.

"Then, we pick up as many Americans as we can, and get up full steam ahead for the west coast. The Panamá Canal was pretty much damaged in the battle with the Purple Fleet,* but

---

* AUTHOR's NOTE: It will be recalled by those who have followed the history of the Purple Invasion that Operator 5 led a flotilla of planes into battle against a huge fleet of the Purple Empire that was about to pass through the Panamá Canal. Several locks of the Canal were destroyed in that battle, but victory crowned the efforts of the American planes. The Purple fleet was entirely annihilated. So great, however, was the power of the Emperor's Armies that the Purple Empire was enabled to complete its conquest of America in spite of the loss of its battle fleet. Now, with the Panamá Canal in the hands of a friendly Central American republic, Operator 5 would

the Republic of Panamá has repaired the locks again. We can make it to Los Angeles in a week. In the meantime we'll radio the Army in Death Valley to march. We'll stake everything on a smashing drive against Los Angeles. The enemy has vast stores of supplies and ammunition there. They've built a network of concrete pill-boxes and trenches that's supposed to be impregnable. Well, if we can capture Los Angeles, it means we can still hope for a free America some day!"

Frank Ames looked dubious. "That's a tall order, Operator 5. The army in Death Valley is ringed around by ten divisions of Marshal Kremer's crack troops. They'll have a tough enough job cutting their way out of there, without taking the offensive against an impregnable position like Los Angeles."

"We'll try it anyway," Jimmy Christopher said. "There's nothing else to do. In the meantime, get to the radio. Keep sending the story of what's just happened—keep sending it all night. Tell all civilians we want them to be ready for a last great effort. When we crash out at Los Angeles, we want the Americans in every city and town and hamlet to rise up at the same time. We'll show Mister Rudolph the First that America still has one good fight left in her!"

Freda Flexner wasn't listening. She had turned away, and was leaning over the rail, with the rain washing her hair. There

encounter no difficulty in passing through. The Central and South American countries had been slow to realize the danger to themselves from the Purple Empire. However, with the spectacle of the Purple excesses in the United States, they were eager to lend him their assistance.

were tears in her eyes. She was thinking of Tim Donovan, small, courageous, alone in New York today, on a mission that would have been dangerous enough for any grown man to quail at!

CHAPTER 6
A MESSAGE FOR
BARON FLEXNER

TIM DONOVAN was thinking of Freda Flexner and of Jimmy Christopher as he silently scaled the bluffs toward the Imperial Palace on the heights overlooking the Hudson River. Those heights had once been known as Fort Tryon Park. They had been the site of the most lovely and the most carefully cultivated bit of ground in New York City. Here, New Yorkers had loved to come of a Sunday morning, to breathe the fresh clear air of the highest spot in the city, and to gaze with wondering eyes at the imposing vista of the Hudson River, winding north and south for miles under their eyes, far below.

But the Purple Invasion had changed all that. Rudolph I had chosen this spot as the site of his new palace. And he had drafted thousands of American civilians in the Forced Labor Corps assigned to the task of building it. Then, declaring with his usual callous smugness that hands which had built his palace must not be employed at any other, lesser task, he had ordered all those workmen hurled to their death over the side of the cliff. At the very place where Tim Donovan had crouched looking up at the lights of the palace, thousands of crushed and mutilated bodies had lain not so long ago. Those bodies had been cleared away to remove the stench of decomposition; but the memory remained with thousands of wives and children whose husbands and fathers did not return home that night.

The recollection of that bloody day stirred within Tim Donovan's breast as he climbed the bluff, careful to avoid making the slightest sound. He knew that sentries would be posted at the top, and he hoped to get by without being challenged. If he were discovered before he succeeded in reaching Baron Flexner, he was determined to sell his life as dearly as possible.

It was a long hard climb, and he was almost out of breath when he reached the top. He dropped flat on his stomach, lay there quietly for a couple of minutes, breathing deeply. The grounds had been changed considerably from the happy carefree days when he had visited Fort Tryon Park as a boy.

A huge, ornate palace reared up toward the heavens where before there had been beautiful trees and shaded walks. A stretch of lawn had been planted in front of the palace, studded with exotic trees that he did not recognize, and with peculiar marble statues. Every window of the palace was lighted, and strains of music floated out through the night. Where the American flag had flown above the bastion of the old fort, there now stood the palace, from whose tower was flaunted the ensign of the Purple Empire, bearing its sinister emblem of the severed head and the crossed broadswords.

There was some kind of reception going on here, and the lad could see men in uniform and women in evening gowns dancing in the ballroom on the main floor. Upstairs would be the Imperial bedroom and the rooms of the members of the court; down below, cut into the body of the rock, would be the dungeons where prisoners never saw the light of day; and in one of those dungeons would be Nan Christopher and Sergeant Aloysius MacTavish. To the left of the palace was a wide, flag-stoned courtyard, and he could discern many figures moving about in the darkness.

He put his hand on the gun in his waistband, and slowly got to his feet, began to move across the lawn. He had spotted a sentry some fifty feet away, and he felt safe, for the man's back was toward him. A quick dash would bring him close to that courtyard where the shadowy figures moved, before the sentry turned.

But he had moved too hastily. Hardly had he taken a dozen steps before a powerful flashlight clicked on at his left, bathing him in light.

A harsh voice barked in the language of the Central Empire: "Halt or die!"

Tim Donovan slid to a stop, his hand slowly easing the gun out of the holster. His young face was determined, his lips set tightly. He had lost his chance. He was discovered. Now he must die fighting.

He waited, hoping that the flashlight would be lowered, so that he could see the patrol that had challenged him. He heard several booted feet approaching, and the sentry at the other end turned and hurried swiftly toward him.

The flashlight was kept steadily in his face, and the voice behind it demanded: "Who are you? What are you doing—*Oh, a leper!*"

Tim shot the cell warden between the eyes.

Tim had forgotten that his face was still begrimed, and that he still wore the scarlet leper's sash. Perhaps there was a chance....

HE KEPT his eyes lowered, and took his hand away from the gun.

The flashlight was clicked off. Now he could distinguish the uniformed Central Empire lieutenant who approached him, followed by two troopers with bayoneted rifles. The lieutenant's voice had lost its harshness. He did not come too close.

"So you are one of the lepers who were invited to the emperor's party? How did you get out here in the grounds?"

Tim Donovan's pulse raced. A party for lepers? Was he playing in luck for a change? It seemed improbable, fantastic, that the cruel, conscienceless Rudolph should have gone to the trouble of entertaining those unfortunates among his subjects who had been stricken with the dread disease. Perhaps this lieutenant was playing with him, like a cat with a mouse. He gripped the gun again, hung his head, but watched the patrol from under lowered lids.

The lieutenant barked again: "Why did you come out here? Why didn't you stay with the others?"

"I—I wanted to look at the grounds, sir," Tim told him.

The lieutenant laughed tolerantly. "Well, you go back with the others. You'll all be given a chance to see the grounds. Better not wander about like this. It is lucky for you that I discovered you, and not the sentry; he would have shot you to death without asking questions. Come this way!"

Tim's eyes glowed as he followed the lieutenant toward the

courtyard where he had seen the shadowy figures. He kept a respectful distance behind the officer, as befitted a lowly unfortunate leper. This was a break he hadn't expected.

That Rudolph I should be sufficiently interested in the sorry condition of the lepers was hardly understandable. However, Tim took it as it came. It gave him his chance to enter the grounds.

The lieutenant led him to a small gate in the fence surrounding the courtyard, and a sentry saluted, stood aside for Tim to pass through. The lieutenant did not enter.

Tim said diffidently: "Thank you, sir."

The lieutenant grinned. "Not at all, leper. It was a pleasure!"

Tim watched the officer walk away, then turned to face the group of lepers who had gathered about him. He saw now that the courtyard was full of them. There must be at least three hundred lepers here.

The boy experienced a feeling of revulsion as the horribly scabrous men came close to him, but he mastered his feelings, and essayed a smile. These men were all gloomy, solemn. Many of them were in the extremely advanced stages of the disease. All of them wore the same kind of scarlet sash that Tim had chosen for his masquerade.

There were Chinese among them, Eurasians, East Indians and half a dozen other assorted races and nationalities. These men had all come over with the Purple troops, and had developed the disease after their arrival. No doubt they had been infected before starting out. But at the first sign of leprosy they had been cast out, to fend for themselves. Most of them had not been in the Purple Army, but had been camp-followers, cooks, and menials. Their lot had indeed been a bitter one, for it had seemed that Rudolph did not care whether they lived or died.

Now, as Tim talked to them, his heart went out to them in sympathy. They were so pathetically glad that something was to be done for them at last.

Tim learned that a proclamation had been posted in the city that morning, inviting all lepers to the palace. They had been in this courtyard most of the day, but so far no one had paid any attention to them, except to wheel in a huge wagon-load of food. They hoped that the emperor would assign some small territory to them, where they could make their home. All they asked was shelter and a little food.

Tim wandered around the courtyard, wondering how he would get out of here to talk to Flexner. There was a low wall separating the yard from the palace proper, and now two huge arc-lights on that wall sprang into life, bathing the courtyard in their brilliance.

On the first floor of the palace, Tim could see the gaily uniformed officers and the beautifully gowned women, standing at the windows and looking down at them. The music inside had stopped, and it seemed that all that gay company was gathering at the windows to watch some performance that was about to start.

The lepers huddled in small groups all around, shielding their eyes against the blaze of the arc-lights. Tim Donovan, glancing around keenly, saw a thing that made his blood run cold. Posted on the towers at either end of the wall were two machine guns.

Troopers were bending over those machine guns, and an officer beside them was looking up toward a window of the palace as if for instruction.

And suddenly Tim Donovan knew the grim, terrible truth!

These lepers were gathered here in the courtyard, not to be helped, not to be fed or housed; *but to be shot!*

RUDOLPH WAS having his bloody jest. He was playing with these unfortunates, leading them to believe that their troubles were to be over. And indeed they were—for the sizzling slugs from those two machine guns would put them out of their misery forever. And characteristically, Rudolph had gathered together his courtiers to make a spectacle of the bloody deed!

The crowded lepers had not yet understood the significance of those machine guns. They probably took them for granted, as part of the defenses of the palace. When that officer got his signal, it would be too late.

And Tim Donovan was trapped with them!

The boy's mind raced swiftly, desperately, from one wild plan to another. The gate at the other end was locked from the outside, and was guarded by sentries. If he warned the lepers, they would try to storm that gate, and be shot down in the attempt. Yet, it might be better to die fighting than to allow themselves to be riddled with lead in supine hopelessness.

The officer on the tower was still looking up impatiently toward the second floor window. Though there were groups of officers and women at all of the windows, there was one at which no revelers stood. And now, as Tim watched, a single figure appeared at that window.

Tim's blood raced. Those purple robes, the high, jewel-studded crown, the cruel mouth and the sharp nose—he had seen those features only once before, but he recognized them. That was Rudolph himself, the Emperor of the Central Empire, Lord of Europe and Asia, conqueror of America. He was going to give the signal which would send the hot lead crashing into the defenseless bodies of these lepers.

The officer on the tower stiffened at sight of the emperor, and saluted, standing at attention. The lepers saw him too, and their shrill talk died down into awed silence. They still had no fore-knowledge of the doom that was awaiting them.

Tim saw the machine-gunners swing the ugly muzzles of their weapons to bear on the courtyard. He saw the men bending over the trips of those guns, awaiting the word that would unleash sudden death. And then, in the hushed silence that had fallen upon the courtyard, Rudolph I began to speak. Behind the emperor there appeared the sallow countenance of Baron Julian Flexner, the father of Freda, and Prime Minister of the Empire. The courtiers at the other windows leaned out to hear better, and the lepers moved closer to the wall unconscious of the deadly menace of the machine guns.

Rudolph's voice was honeyed at first, and Tim could detect the hidden sneer as he spoke.

"You lepers," he began, "have been living miserably. You have had little to eat, and in many cases no place to sleep. People shun you for fear of catching your disease. Yet you have done no harm to anyone. It is a pity that you should live and suffer so."

There were glad murmurs from the lepers. The emperor sympathized with them! At last they were to be helped!

Their murmurs died down as Rudolph went. "We have been thinking about your sorry condition, and we have reached a decision. It is not fitting that in such a great Empire as ours, there should be a class of men like you. We have decided, therefore, to end your misery!"

The lepers uttered a low cheer.

Rudolph's voice suddenly hardened, and his next words smote them like a sledgehammer: "No longer shall you filthy carriers of disease walk the streets; no longer shall you beg for bread and alms. Your misery ends tonight—now. You are all to be shot—and your troubles will be over!"

Rudolph's announcement was greeted by a stunned silence from the lepers. Their minds refused to grasp the significance of it. They could not believe that the emperor who had begun his speech to them in such a kindly fashion should have planned this dreadful thing for them.

But the courtiers at the other windows enjoyed the jest in full. Laughter echoed from the palace. This was indeed a huge joke; and the spectacle of these lepers being slaughtered would spice their satiated appetite for sensations.

And now the lepers understood that they were to die. They looked at the machine guns, saw the officer waiting for the signal from Rudolph, saw the troopers bending over the trips, and knew that death was only a moment away.

They began to utter shrill screams of fear, and to mill around in the courtyard, pressing frantically toward the locked gate at the far side. The yard became a bedlam of terror.

AND STILL Rudolph did not give the word to fire. He was waiting, savoring to the full the terror and panic of these unfortunate men. He was bending forward, eager-eyed, trying to catch every phase of emotion of these poor victims of his.

Tim Donovan's lips pressed tightly together. His hand stole to his waistband, came up with the automatic he had concealed there. That window was a good distance away, and he would have to fire upward, at an angle, in the face of the glare of the arc-lights. But he was going to try.

He was going to try to kill the emperor!

Though Tim Donovan was a very good shot, the chances of success were slim. That blinding arc-light alone was a great handicap. And he knew that he wouldn't have more than one shot. Those machine-guns would begin to spit the moment he fired. But the lad didn't count the odds.

Standing there almost alone, while the lepers were storming the gate, Tim raised his automatic, flipped off the safety, and lined the emperor's face in his sights, He could barely distinguish Rudolph, but he fired.

The shot crashed out in the night, drowning for an instant the frenzied screams of the lepers and the laughter of the courtiers.

Tim Donovan saw Rudolph jerk, saw him put a hand to his shoulder, and twist away from the window. Bitterly, Tim knew that though he had hit the Emperor, he had not killed him.

The officer on the tower uttered a shout of rage. The courtiers began to shout and gesticulate, pointing at Tim.

"That's the one!" they screamed. "That's the one who shot the Emperor!"

The lepers had swung from their futile attempts to crash the gate, and they came running back, shrieking, waving their arms. The officer on the tower turned toward his machine-gun crew, was about to issue a swift order to fire. But before he could speak, Tim Donovan shot him through the head. The officer threw up his arms, toppled backward off the wall.

The machine-gunners were dazed, but they mechanically swung their gun toward Tim, and one of them bent to the trips. The gun in the other tower was likewise turned upon the lad.

But now the lepers, maddened with terror, and realizing that they would all be slaughtered if they remained here, swarmed toward the wall, and began to boost each other up. The machine-gunners, without the authority of an officer, changed their minds about firing at Tim, and deflected the muzzles of their weapons to rake the climbing lepers.

Tim Donovan was grinning mirthlessly as he raised his automatic, aimed carefully, and picked off the two men at the trips of the two guns. The rapid-firers remained silent, and a second trooper jumped to replace the men whom Tim had shot. But by now the foremost of the lepers had reached the top of the wall, and they swarmed over, screaming, clawing, kicking, gouging. They literally overwhelmed the gunners, and the unfortunate Central Empire troopers were hurled from the wall.

The lepers sent up a shout of victory. They commanded the palace from the two towers. Almost as one man, they looked toward Tim Donovan for orders.

Now two of their number, still in the courtyard, cupped their hands and boosted him up to the top. He could see troopers with rifles running toward the courtyard from several directions, and he issued swift directions. In a moment the lepers had swung one of the guns around to pepper away at the approaching troopers, while the other rapid-firer was set to cover the palace windows. Many of the courtiers who had remained standing at those windows now hastened to get out of range.

Tim sent two shots into the two great arc-lights at either end of the wall, and plunged the whole courtyard into darkness.

"You can hold this place for a long time now," he told them. "There's plenty of ammunition here, and the troopers can only come at you through that gate. Keep the gate covered, and don't be afraid to shoot. If any one shows himself at the windows of the palace, pepper them!"

"Where are you going?" one of the lepers asked him.

"I've got an appointment in there," Tim told him grimly. "Wait till I come back, if you can. If not, take the machine-guns and cut your way to the foot of the cliff."

He tore the scarlet sash from his waist, and leaped down off the wall into the narrow passage just outside the palace.

The machine-gun above him began to stutter once more, as the lepers mowed down the first contingent of troopers to come through the gate.

TIM DIDN'T look back. He hastened along the alley, and found a small door in the palace wall. He tried it, found it open, and slipped inside. He found himself in a brilliantly lighted corridor, with people scurrying about in wild disorder. Importantly uniformed men were issuing orders which no one obeyed. A panic seemed to be spreading among the courtiers. None of them knew whether the Emperor had been killed, or only wounded. Tim heard some one say that Baron Flexner had taken Rudolph upstairs to the Imperial bedroom, and the lad hastened across the corridor, found a broad staircase. Guards were running around aimlessly, and men and women were talking excitedly in small groups, while others peered furtively out of the windows at the battle going on outside.

The clatter of the machine guns had become almost continuous now, and Tim Donovan knew that the lepers would be attacked by every available trooper in New York. Within an hour there would be an unbreakable cordon around the palace. Not one of those lepers would escape death. In the meantime, the boy stuck to his original intention; so far he had escaped death by a miracle, and he intended to keep on, until he either succeeded in rescuing Nan and MacTavish, or was killed.

No one paid any attention to him as he sped up the stairs to the upper floor. There were more courtiers and attendants on this floor, and there was a small crowd down at the end of the corridor in front of the Imperial bedroom. A dozen of the Imperial Household Guards were on duty at the door, and a physician was pushing through the crowd of courtiers.

The door of the bedroom opened, and Baron Flexner came out, held the door open for the physician to enter. Tim Donovan had inserted another clip in his automatic, and he kept it under his waistband, ready to draw if he were challenged. His appearance, even without the sash, was disreputable enough to have caused him to be stopped before he took a single step, had it not been for the general excitement.

He had wiped some of the grime and mud from his face, but his clothes were still dirty and torn.

Baron Flexner glanced down the hall, and his keen gaze settled upon Tim. The Baron stiffened. He remembered the lad from previous encounters, and he recognized him at once. Tim had deliberately placed himself in a position where Flexner could spot him, otherwise he would never have been able to reach the Baron.

Flexner's eyes narrowed, and he spoke a few words to one of the Household Guards at the door. Then the Baron pushed through the crowd, headed directly for Tim, with the guard following. From the outside they could still hear the sharp staccato rapping of the two machine-guns. The battle was raging out there, and the lepers, desperate in their knowledge that defeat meant death, must be putting up a good fight.

Flexner paid no attention to the din coming from the courtyard. His thin lips were pressed into a tight line as he advanced upon Tim. The guard behind him had cocked his rifle, and held it so that it covered the lad.

Tim did not waver, but waited stiffly for Flexner to come close to him.

FLEXNER STOPPED ten paces away, and smiled thinly. "You shot His Imperial Majesty. You are Tim Donovan. You must be mad to have come into the palace. You know what will be done to you?"

Tim's eyes were fearless. "I imagine there must be some very special punishment reserved for anyone who dares to shoot His Imperial Majesty," he said. "I'm sure your ingenuity will devise something extra painful."

The guard had stopped out of earshot, but with his rifle still covering Tim. Flexner appeared puzzled. "You are a foolhardy boy—more so even than your friend, Operator 5. One would almost think that you had deliberately placed yourself here so that I would see you—"

"Exactly, Baron," Tim broke in. "You see, I have a message to deliver to you. Read this, please. It will explain everything."

Still puzzled, Flexner took the letter which Tim handed him. He opened it, frowning, and glanced without understanding at the single lock of golden hair that fell into his hand. Then he unfolded the letter, and his face became white as he read:

Dear Father:

I am the prisoner of these barbarous Americans whom you have so often warned me against. Operator 5 is in command of them, and he is a very ruthless man. He instructs me to tell you that if his sister, Nan, and Sergeant MacTavish do not return to him with the boy who is bringing you this message, I will be made to pay the penalty. Father, they will surely kill me if you do not contrive to release Nan Christopher and Sergeant MacTavish. They say that they will cut off my head and send it to you in a box. Dear father, please don't let them kill me!

Freda.

Flexner's hand was trembling. He crushed the letter, staring at the lock of golden hair. "My daughter! Freda!" he groaned.

Tim was watching him with commiserating eyes. He understood how this man felt.

Baron Julian Flexner was Prime Minister of the Purple Empire; as such, his power was second only to that of Rudolph himself. And he had not used that power sparingly. Flexner had willingly—nay, almost eagerly—carried out many of the depraved ideas of the sadistic Emperor whom he served. He had caused the death of thousands, the torture of millions more. He had permitted his soldiers to rape and pillage throughout the Occupied Territory. That little severed finger which Tim Donovan had seen this day could only be attributed to the fact that Flexner had permitted and encouraged the troopers of the Purple Empire to indulge in any excesses of cruelty that took their fancy.

Baron Flexner had never counted the misery of those who were unfortunate enough to fall under his power. A mother's bereavement had meant nothing to him; the lives of those poor lepers who were fighting desperately meant nothing to him.

But now—now he was faced with a dose of the same medicine. His own daughter was threatened with the same fate that had overtaken thousands of Americans. And even though it was a sort of retributive justice, Tim felt sorry for the man.

"I assure you that your daughter will not be harmed, Baron," he said, "if you comply with the demands of Operator 5. I am authorized to give you his word on that."

Flexner was glancing around like a trapped beast. He made sure that the guard was out of earshot, then asked huskily: "W-what does he want me to do?"

Tim replied quickly: "You are to manage the escape of Nan Christopher and Sergeant MacTavish. You are to help them and me get to the Jersey coast, where we will be picked up. If you do that, your daughter will be returned to you, unharmed, within two days!"

Crowds were thronging the hall now, and many were glancing curiously at the ragged individual with whom the Prime Minister was conversing. Outside the rattle of musketry mingled with the *rat-tat-tat* of the machine guns. At the end of the corridor, the Imperial Physician was tending to Rudolph's wound in the Imperial bedroom.

But these two paid no attention to anyone or anything but each other. Tim was watching Flexner closely, wondering whether the other would yield. Would he guess that Operator 5 was only bluffing? Would he be a clever enough student of human nature to understand that Operator 5 could never bring himself to harm a young and innocent girl like Freda? Would he refuse to accede to Tim's demands, and stake everything on his knowledge of human nature?

On the other hand, Flexner was staring at Tim Donovan, fingering the lock of his daughter's hair, while sweat rolled down his high, glistening forehead. His daughter was in the hands of the enemy. He thought of the many dreadful things that had been done in the Occupied Territory with his sanction. He thought of Nan Christopher, down in the dungeon below the palace. And though he was a shrewd and clever diplomat, he judged other men by himself. He imagined how he would feel, what he would do, if he were Operator 5 and if his sister were

tortured and executed wantonly—and if he had in his hands the daughter of the man who was partially responsible for that torture and execution.

Suddenly his thin lips twitched. "M-my daughter will be returned safely? Operator 5 promises it?"

Tim nodded, restraining his eagerness.

"Operator 5 promises it. And he always keeps his word, as you know."

"I—know!" Flexner groaned. "But how can I release Nan

Christopher and the sergeant? If Rudolph discovered it, he would have me crucified!"

"That is something for you to figure out, Baron," Tim told him. "You should be able to get away with it."

Flexner hesitated a second, while the battle raged outside. Then he said abruptly: "Follow me!"

CHAPTER 7
THE BARON PLAYS GUIDE

THE BARON led the way along the corridor, pushing past the wondering groups of courtiers. Tim followed him, hand on the butt of his automatic. He was successful so far; but there was no telling what swift emergency might arise.

The guard trailed after them. Flexner motioned to him imperiously, and the man fell back.

Tim followed the Baron down the broad stairway to the main floor. Here, troopers were at every window, sniping at the lepers on the wall. All the windows were broken, and machine-gun slugs were sweeping the floor as the lepers kept up a continuous barrage of lead. The troopers had to fire at an angle, to avoid being hit themselves, and the courtiers and attendants had all fled to inner rooms to avoid the steel-jacketed slugs that swept the floor, ricocheting dangerously.

Flexner and Tim dashed across the floor to the rear, and they barely missed being hit. Flexner darted into a narrow corridor, followed by Tim. He opened a huge oak door, revealing a steep staircase that led down into semi-darkness.

At the bottom of those stairs, Tim gazed in wonder at the rows of barred cell doors. Small ten-watt bulbs illuminated this cellar of dungeons, affording just enough light to see the pallid faces of the prisoners in the rows of cells. All those prisoners were silent, with their faces pressed close to the bars. They had heard the shooting upstairs, and they wondered who was bold enough to attack the Imperial Palace, in the heart of the Purple territory. They entertained little hope of being rescued, but they were praying with all their hearts that whoever was up there fighting the Purple troops should not be captured and brought down here to join them as prisoners.

These Americans in the cells all knew what fate awaited them. They, with Nan Christopher and Sergeant MacTavish, were to be crucified on Coronation Day. And they were determined to die without a plea for mercy, without affording the sadistic Rudolph the satisfaction of seeing that they were afraid. Now, at sight of Flexner and Tim, they still maintained absolute silence, but watched every move of the two.

Flexner led the way through the cold stone corridor, then turned to the right, following another corridor also lined with occupied cells. Tim did not speak to any of the prisoners who were watching their passage. He was taut, on guard lest Flexner try some last-minute bit of treachery—though he felt that the Baron would go through with it now, for his daughter's sake.

Flexner confirmed this feeling by turning to him and whispering: "I don't know how I am going to accomplish this thing. The Cell Warden is in sole charge down here at night, and he takes orders from no one but the Emperor. Not even I have any authority over him."

"Why is that?" Tim asked.

"Because the Cell Warden is also the official Palace Executioner. He amuses himself at night by torturing some of the prisoners."

"I'd like to meet the gentleman!" Tim said grimly.

He followed the other along a third corridor, and marveled at the number of cells down here. If all these prisoners were to be crucified on Coronation Day, Rudolph must have been planning a spectacle of agony on the grand scale.

At one point in the corridor there was a spot where there were cells on only one side. The other side was a vast open space, where large cases were stacked one upon the other, almost to the ceiling.

"What are those cases?" Tim asked.

"They are supplies for the Household Guards," Flexner explained. "They contain uniforms, arms and ammunition. The Household Guards have a separate Commissary—*there's the cell!*"

HE STOPPED short, pointing to a cell on the right, the door of which was open. Low sounds of brutish laughter came from within that cell, followed by a cool, hard voice uttering phlegmatic curses.

"Damn you, you cold-blooded fiend! Let that girl alone! If I could get my hands out of these bracelets I'd twist your damned head off your damned neck!"

Tim Donovan recognized that cool voice, and a thrill ran

98

down his spine. "MacTavish!" he exclaimed under his breath. He ran forward noiselessly on his toes, came abreast of the open cell door.

He came to an abrupt stop, staring into the cell. His young face hardened into grim lines. What he saw there sent his hand darting toward the automatic in his waistband.

Nan Christopher and Sergeant Aloysius MacTavish were shackled with their back to the cell wall. Standing before them, and chuckling wickedly, was the gross figure of the Cell Warden. He held a long bayoneted rifle, and he was amusing himself by prodding Nan Christopher's white body with the point.

Little trickles of blood were running down Nan's side. The Cell Warden had just jerked the bayonet out, and Tim could see that only the extreme tip was red with blood.

The brute chuckled again, said: "Each time it will go a little deeper, my fine girl. After a few more days of this, your body will be a fine sight when it is placed upon the cross. After all, this is for your benefit. It will harden you to stand the agonies of crucifixion!"

Sergeant MacTavish, shackled alongside Nan, began to curse again. "You dirty coward!" He tugged ineffectually at the shackles, his powerful shoulder muscles standing out in ridges under the strain. "Leave that girl alone! If I ever get loose—"

"Stop, Mac," Nan Christopher gasped. "I—can take it!"

The Cell Warden chuckled. "Your big friend talks loud, my fine girl. I will soon work on him—"

He stopped, suddenly sensing the presence of Tim. The big

brute swung around, saw the lad standing in the doorway, and at the same instant Nan and Mac saw the lad.

"Timmy!" Nan exclaimed.

MacTavish groaned. "Now they've got the kid, too!"

"No, Mac," Tim Donovan said tightly. "They haven't got me. Baron Flexner here—" he motioned toward the Baron, who had come up alongside him—"has suddenly had a change of heart. He is going to free you!"

Several of the American prisoners in the other cells heard what Tim said, and a low cheer went up from them. "More power to you, boy!" they called out.

The Cell Warden glared at Tim and Flexner, holding his bloody, dripping bayonet at the ready. "What are you doing here, Baron?" he demanded. "You know the Emperor's rules—no one but me is permitted in the dungeons at night!"

Tim's eyes were hard, unrelenting. "Stand aside!" he ordered.

Sergeant MacTavish suddenly laughed loud and long. "Boy, this is going to be a pleasure. Wait till my hands are free—will I go to work on that damned fiend!"

The Cell Warden glared at MacTavish, then at Flexner. "You are mad!" he said to the Baron. "The Emperor will have you crucified!"

Flexner shrugged. "I cannot help that, Tauglitz. I must ask you to release these prisoners!"

Tauglitz's small pig eyes narrowed. "So? We shall see!"

And with a sudden swift movement that was exceedingly fast for so large a man, he lunged with his bayonet at Tim Donovan.

But the lad was prepared for that move; indeed, he had hoped that the Cell Warden would do something like that. His automatic came out from under his waistband with a lightning-quick movement, and he shot the Cell Warden between the eyes.

The man screamed once—a scream that was choked off almost before it began; and he pitched forward on his face, with the rifle underneath him. He lay still on the floor at the boy's feet. Tim's lips were trembling. He looked down at the man he had just killed, then said to Flexner: "Maybe it's better this way, Baron. Now there will be no one to tell the Emperor who freed the prisoners."

MacTAVISH WAS cursing again, but this time quietly. "Dammit, kid, did you have to kill him? You should have saved him for me. Shooting was too good for that swine. Look what he's been doing to Nan!"

MacTavish was only talking for the purpose of relieving the strain. He saw that Nan's eyes were brimming with tears, and that her slender, white body was trembling with the reaction. In a moment she might become hysterical; and this was no time for hysterics.

Nan tightened under MacTavish's effort to divert her attention. She looked over at the sergeant. "It's all right, Mac, you don't have to worry about me. I won't snap!"

They both watched Tim searching through the pockets of the dead Cell Warden, saw him come up triumphantly with a set of keys. Flexner stood by, saying nothing, while Tim tried the keys in the locks of their shackles, finally succeeded in opening them.

Nan slumped to the floor when she was released, and covered her face with her hands. She began to sob. Most of the clothing had been torn from her body, and the red welts of the bayonet pricks shone up starkly against her white skin.

MacTavish, as soon as the shackles fell from him, stepped over and raised her to her feet, put an arm around her. "Buck up, Nan. We've got to get out of here!"

He turned, grasped Tim's hand. "Kid, I got to hand it to you. You have guts, to come in here after us. And how come Baron Flexner here is aiding and abetting?"

Sketchily, Tim explained about Freda.

Then: "And now it's up to the Baron to get us out of here, and over to the Jersey shore. What about it, Baron?"

Flexner wiped perspiration from his forehead. "I have already done enough to warrant my crucifixion. What more can I do? How can I get you out past the troopers outside? They are battling the lepers, and there will be hundreds of troopers surrounding the palace. You could never get through the cordon—"

He broke off, staring at Tim Donovan. The boy had snapped his fingers in sudden glee, and his eyes were shining with inspiration. He held up a huge key, one of the dozen or so on the ring he had taken from Tauglitz's body.

"I bet this is the key to all these cell doors! We can release every last American in these dungeons!"

Flexner began to protest. "Wait! That is not in our bargain! You were to have only these two. The others must remain—"

"The devil with the bargain!" Tim Donovan snapped. "Do you think we're going to leave all these men to be crucified? Nix!"

He sped from cell to cell, turning the key in lock after lock, calling to the bewildered prisoners: "Come on out, everybody!"

Flexner hurried after him, followed by Nan and Mac. Flexner was sweating profusely now. He gripped Tim by the elbow. "But how will you escape? There are more than a hundred prisoners here. You will be caught. How can you all get through our troops? My God, you will all be captured, and my daughter will die—"

MacTavish gripped him by the arm. "Forget it, Flexner. The kid knows what he's doing. I bet he's got a stunt all figured out!"

And indeed he had.

After all the cell doors were unlocked, the prisoners thronged in the corridor. From up above the sounds of firing came to them dully because of the thickness of the walls. The battle was still going on up there.

Tim led all the American prisoners to the storeroom where he had seen the cases of supplies, pointed to them proudly. "Break them open!" he said. "Put on the uniforms! We'll march out of here as Imperial Household Guards—and by golly, we'll get de luxe transportation to the Jersey shore!"

The prisoners uttered cheer after cheer as the audacity of the plan became clear to them. They were willing to take any risks, for here in the dungeons, only certain death awaited them. Armed with the rifles and revolvers in those cases, and equipped with Purple Empire uniforms, they would have a fair chance of escaping; or of fighting for their lives at least, if they should be discovered.

As the prisoners donned their uniforms and equipped themselves with arms, Sergeant MacTavish lined them up in column of fours in the corridor. Many of these prisoners were famous Americans. Among them were the mayors of dozens of cities, who had been especially brought here to be made part of the Coronation spectacle. There were several judges, as well as other men who had once occupied a high position in American arts and letters, politics and business.

They made a goodly showing. Sergeant MacTavish, looking them over, was surprised to note that all of them were shaved, and that they had fresh haircuts. One of the men explained to him that they had been favored with the attentions of a barber by Imperial order, so that they would make a nice appearance for the Coronation.

Nan Christopher and Tim also donned uniforms, and joined the ranks. Then, MacTavish waved to Baron Flexner. "You can go up first, Baron. I think I can trust you not to give the alarm?" Flexner nodded slowly. His eyes were fixed in silent admiration upon Tim Donovan, who stood in the first rank.

"You are indeed a clever boy," he said. "I have never seen anyone like you. I—I almost hope you get through—and not for my daughter's sake!"

Tim gave him a tight smile. "Thanks, Baron. And rest assured that your daughter will be promptly returned to you."

MacTavish glanced proudly down the length of the column. "What a gang!" he murmured. "Why don't we try to capture the Emperor?"

Flexner started perceptibly. "My God! Are you not satisfied with what you have already accomplished? I must tell you that the Emperor is no longer in the palace. The physician who came to see him was arranging to have him moved immediately from the palace. His Majesty has only a slight shoulder wound, but he cannot stand the sounds of the battle that is going on outside. He has no doubt already been moved to a quieter spot!"

"Where to?" MacTavish demanded tightly.

Flexner smiled. "I would never tell you. You could cut me to pieces, but you would never learn from me!"

MacTavish shrugged. "We won't cut you to pieces, mister. We're too anxious to get away. Go on up ahead of us. We'll give you three minutes to get out of the way, then we'll march out. Order the troops outside to stop firing at the lepers. We'll take those poor chaps along with us, out of reach of the Emperor's revenge!"

Flexner bowed stiffly. "Trust me. And the next time we meet, I shall see to it that you do not have the upper hand!"

He turned and walked swiftly up the stairs....

CHAPTER 8
THE KONDOR PUTS TO SEA

THAT NIGHT, the battleship *Kondor*, standing off the Jersey shore, resembled a gray wraith in the darkness. The coast line lay low and bleak, set off by the white foam of the breakers. Rain slashed down in slanting sheets upon the angry waters of the Atlantic, and washed the decks of the great ship.

The Purple Empire crew of the *Kondor* had been set ashore hours ago. They had shown no disposition to dispute possession of the ship with the Americans. Jimmy Christopher had long ago noticed that the Purple soldiers were almost invincible when they marched in perfect discipline under adequate leadership, and accompanied by the powerful guns, tanks and planes with which Rudolph had equipped them; but once remove those advantages, deprive them of the support of the mechanized units that cleared the way for them, and the Purple troopers lost their heart for battle. When the odds on their side were reduced, they were no longer the formidable soldiers that had marched to conquest under the sinister emblem of the severed head and the crossed broadswords.

This was equally true of the naval forces. Rudolph's seamen were brave in their new, powerful battleships and cruisers that could outrange and out-sail anything on the five seas. But at hand-to-hand conflict the Americans could beat them every time.

And it was not strange that it should be so. These men were recruited from every part of the world, from the slums of Europe and the East, and from the jails of the Continent. They marched because of the iron discipline of the Purple Armies; they fought because they knew that victory would give them the chance to loot, to pillage, to rape. But they had no burning cause for which to fight; they had no ideal for which they would be glad to die.

The capture of the *Kondor* had demonstrated that. The Americans had been courageously ready to touch off the case of *electro-thermite*, and to die with the enemy; but the Central Empire marines and crew had not been willing. They had supinely laid down their arms and surrendered.

Now, Operator 5 was handling the great ship with a short crew. If they should be sighted by any unit of the Purple Empire Atlantic Fleet, they would be open to destruction, for there was not sufficient man-power aboard to handle the ship and the guns at the same time. But every man on board was fiercely resolved, if they should be spotted and attacked, to fight until they sank.

And Jimmy Christopher had taken steps to remedy that shortage of skilled gunners and able seamen. Even now, Frank Ames was in the radio room, broadcasting an appeal to all undercover American amateur radio stations. He was using a prearranged method of distortion, which safeguarded the message from being intercepted by the enemy.

"Flash this news to all Americans!" he was saying. "Operator 5 has destroyed four new battleships of the Purple Empire at the Hog Island Shipyards. He has also destroyed the enemy powder plants at Philadelphia, and captured the Purple Empire battleship, *Kondor*. We are standing off Atlantic City on the Jersey shore, and are urgently in need of volunteer seamen and gunners, also engineers. Those Americans who wish to volunteer are urged to make their way to Atlantic City and signal from the shore; code—three, two, one, three, with a flashlight. We will put off boats to take them aboard. I will now repeat...."

And so he droned on interminably, reporting the news of the brilliant *coup*. And throughout America, amateur radios hidden in cellars, in lofts, in haystacks, picked up his message. Then those operators went forth into the night to spread the news, to relay Operator 5's appeal for volunteers.

Civilians everywhere within traveling distance of Atlantic City said good-bye to wives and children, and stole out, dodging enemy patrols, to make their way to the coast. Seamen, gunners, ex-navy men who had long ago retired because of age or disability, seized this opportunity to escape from the Occupied Territory and to take one more fling at the enemy.

All night long flashlights blinked on the shore—three, two, one, three. And all night long boats put off from the *Kondor* to bring fresh volunteers. These men all knew that they were embarking on a perilous journey, from which they might never return. But they had sweated long enough under the lash of the Purple taskmasters, and they welcomed the chance for liberty or death.

Before dawn, the ship's complement was complete. Operator 5 had a full crew, and he was ready to do battle with any unit of the Purple Navy. Those volunteers, exhibiting great forethought, had brought with them what little supplies of food they could gather. And cans of corned beef, beans, soup, and other foods poured into the ship's storehouse.

The stores—were ample anyway, for the Central Empire had been careful to equip its ships well; but these voluntary gifts would make it possible for the *Kondor* to cruise for a long time without having to raid for supplies. There was ample store of fuel aboard to run its Diesel engines for twenty thousand miles, and the ship was equipped with a giant distillator to make fresh drinking water from the ocean. The *Kondor* would be virtually self-sufficient for months.

BUT JIMMY CHRISTOPHER, standing on the bridge

with his binoculars fixed upon the shore, did not feel any great elation. He was thinking of Tim Donovan, and castigating himself with bitter recriminations.

Freda Flexner stood beside him, her slender fingers twisting and untwisting a small lace handkerchief. She too was staring toward the shore, regardless of the rain that laved her face, and of the wind that was whipping her blonde hair behind her so that she looked like some young Viking woman from an ancient galley of the Norsemen.

"I should never have let the kid go!" Jimmy Christopher said bitterly. "If anything happens to him, I'll never forgive myself. The job is a big one for a grown man—let alone a boy. Even if he succeeds in forcing your father to help in releasing Nan and Mac, there's still the job of getting here."

Freda stirred uneasily. She raised her wide, blue eyes to Jimmy's. "You—love him very much, do you not?" she asked throatily.

Jimmy nodded. "I feel like a big brother to him. Tim Donovan has been with me for so long that—that life would seem empty to me without him."

"And for me, too, life would be empty!" Freda Flexner said. She put a hand on his sleeve, went on impulsively. "Do not laugh at me, Operator 5. You will say that I am only a child, and do not know what love is. But I am almost sixteen, and I know my heart and my mind. I would want nothing better than to stay with you Americans, and to be at Tim's side forever. I—do not want to go back to my father. You—you will let me stay here, Operator 5? I beg you—"

Suddenly, Jimmy Christopher tensed. He gazed tensely through the binoculars.

"Look at that!" he exclaimed. "There's a whole company of Purple Empire troopers marching along the shore! My God, I hope they're not going to attack us. It would be suicide on their part. We could wipe them out with a couple of well-placed shells!"

Freda strained her eyes toward the shore, while Jimmy watched through the glass. He saw the company of troopers draw up on the beach, saw some one who looked like their commanding officer step forward, accompanied by two other, smaller figures.

Operator 5 was puzzled. "Evidently they want to talk to us. What—"

He stopped as a flashlight in the hands of one of those figures on shore began to flicker on and off: *three, two, one, three.*

"It's the signal!" he exclaimed. "More volunteers. Though where they got the uniforms is more than I can understand—"

Frank Ames had come up on the bridge from the radio room. "Be careful, Operator 5," he warned. "It may be a trap to get our boats ashore. Maybe the Purple Intelligence picked up my broadcast, and sent these troops—"

"No, no!" Jimmy Christopher almost shouted. "It's Tim—Tim. Donovan and Nan, and Mac! Look—he's clicking the flashlight in Morse code! Wait—let me get the message!"

The smaller of the three figures on the beach was flashing his torch on and off, in long and short dots and dashes. Jimmy Christopher followed those symbols with the familiarity of one who was thoroughly at home with Morse. He had trained Tim Donovan as well as the others of his small band, to send and receive both Morse and International with the same ease that they used in speaking English. Now he had no difficulty in interpreting the message:

"Operator 5! Operator 5! Tim Donovan, MacTavish and Nan calling. We have two hundred men here, ready to come aboard. Send boats!"

Jimmy Christopher translated the message to Freda and Ames, and Freda's eyes became wet with tears of joy. Jimmy himself allowed no trace of emotion to show in his face at the news that his sister and MacTavish were safe. But he began to issue swift orders that galvanized the crew into action.

"Lower the boats!" he shouted. "Every boat is to put off. There are two hundred men coming aboard!"

"Holy mackerel!" Frank Ames exclaimed. "That kid, Tim, is a cockeyed wonder! Not only does he bring back Nan and Mac, but he brings a small army in the bargain!"

IT WAS almost an hour before the last of those two hundred escaped prisoners clambered aboard. Nan Christopher huddled in her brother's arms.

"Jimmy!" she gasped, "I—I never expected to leave that palace except to be crucified. And—Tim did it. He got us out!"

Freda Flexner and Tim Donovan were talking earnestly in a corner near the chart house. Jimmy Christopher smiled, and let them alone. He did not need to congratulate the boy, to tell him what a fine job he had done. For between those two there was very little need of speech. This boy and this man understood

111

each other so well, that words were utterly unnecessary. And no words that Jimmy could have uttered would have expressed the depth of his feelings.

He thought this as he eyed Tim, talking earnestly to Freda. What could he say? Could he say: "I'm glad you're safe, Tim?" Could he say: "That was a swell job you did, Tim?" Could he say: "You don't know how worried I was about you?"

All those things, and much more, had been expressed in the first moment that Operator 5 had helped the lad over the side, and had clasped hands with him. Their eyes had met for a long minute, and then Tim Donovan had smiled with satisfaction, and Jimmy had squeezed his hand hard. That was all—and it was enough.

Now Jimmy Christopher knew that a hard moment was coming for Tim and Freda. She must go back to her father, and they must say good-bye. It had been promised, and the promise must be kept, whether Freda wanted to go or not. Flexner had kept his part of the bargain, according to Tim's story. Tim had quickly told Operator 5 how Flexner had taken him down to the dungeons, how Tim had killed the Cell Warden and released the prisoners. He had told how Flexner had gone up ahead of the newly formed company of pseudo-household guards, and had ordered the cessation of fighting. Then, MacTavish had led them out, had gone through the mummery of making prisoners of all the lepers.

Those unfortunates had permitted it when Tim Donovan told them who they were. And then they had commandeered autos and trucks, and had ridden away toward the Jersey shore. In a little valley near the Raritan River they had left the lepers. The spot had been a secret headquarters of American undercover workers, and it was well stocked with food, hard to discover. The lepers would be safe there for a long time.

Jimmy watched Tim and Freda for a while, then, reluctantly, he approached them. "I'm sorry kids," he said, "but time's up. You've got to go back to your father, Freda."

The girl had been crying. She clung to Tim. "I—I don't want to go back. Can't I stay here?"

Jimmy shook his head. "Your father risked his honor and his head to ransom you. You can't let him down, Freda."

She hung her head, realizing the cogency of the argument. Tim said: "Freda, I hate to let you go. But I promised your father. Some day, when peace is restored in America, I'll come looking for you. I swear it."

"And I'll wait for you, Tim!" Her childish face, with its wealth of childish beauty, robbed her words of any hint of melodrama. She spoke sincerely, and she meant it. "Oh, why do we have to be enemies? Why does my father have to serve the Emperor, who hates America? Why must men seek to conquer and to kill other men?" She buried her head on Tim's shoulder, and cried.

At last she composed herself, and climbed down the ladder to the boat that was waiting for her. Three men went with her. They had volunteered to conduct her back to a spot where she could get in touch with a Purple Empire patrol.

By taking her back to shore, these men were giving up their opportunity of serving with the *Kondor,* and they did it reluctantly. Finally, however, the boat put off, and Jimmy and Tim and Nan watched it reach shore. Jimmy put a hand on Tim's shoulder.

"I hope, kid," he said huskily, "that you find her again!"

Tim said nothing. He did not take his eyes from the shore.

And now, all the lethargy was gone from Operator 5. He rang the signal for all hands to stand by, and then addressed the crew by means of the public address system of loudspeakers which were distributed throughout the ship so that the captain could talk to every man aboard simultaneously.

"Men, we've taken the first step toward freeing America from the Purple Conquest. We have accomplished a good deal in the last twenty-four hours, but that is only a drop in the bucket to what faces us. We're sailing for the west coast. We're sailing to launch a major attack upon an important enemy stronghold. If we succeed, there won't be any stopping us. If we fail, America is doomed.

"We are going to attack Los Angeles. The enemy has vast stores of supplies and ammunition there. But it's strongly fortified. They've dug in all around in the hills surrounding Los Angeles, and they have a network of concrete pillboxes and trenches. But we have an army of a hundred thousand men in Death Valley. I'm going to issue the order by radio for that army to attack Los Angeles. We'll sail through the Canal, and attack from the sea. As you know, the enemy has no fleet at the present time in Pacific waters, since we destroyed their armada at the Battle of the Farallon Islands.* We'll have the ocean to ourselves. But they'll send their whole Atlantic Fleet after us when they learn where we are; and they'll throw all their shock troops into the Los Angeles district against our Death Valley Army. The odds against us are going to be terrific, but the stakes are big. *Are you game?*"

For a moment there was silence, and then, from every corner of the rain-swept deck there came a long, joyous shout: "Let's go, Operator 5!"

Jimmy Christopher smiled in the darkness. He turned and pushed the engine-room signal *"Full Speed Ahead!"*

---

* AUTHOR'S NOTE: It will be recalled that the Battle of the Farallon Islands was one of the high spots in the record of the Purple Invasion. Those were the dark days when America was fighting with her back to the Rockies, with only a narrow strip of seacoast still unconquered by the Purple Empire. It was then that Emperor Rudolph launched a huge battle fleet across the Pacific, against San Francisco. Equipped with great guns, larger than any before seen on the sea, this armada would wipe San Francisco off the map, land enough troops to take the American Defense Force in the rear. It was in this emergency that Operator 5 led a flotilla of planes out to do battle with the enemy fleet. The result of that battle can be read in any history book. The enemy fleet was entirely destroyed, and San Francisco was saved. Thus, the Purple Empire at this time had no ships in the Pacific and the coast would be clear for the *Kondor's* operations.

CHAPTER 9
DEATH VALLEY

O N A ridge of the Panamint Mountains overlooking Death Valley, a lone American sentry stood guard. He was facing west, and from where he stood he could command a clear view of the Mojave Desert for miles and miles.

The white sand of the Mojave was spotted with myriad tents, and with the figures of bustling men whose helmets glinted in the hot sun. Tanks and armored motorcycles too numerous to count sat on the sand in mutely threatening formation. And over certain of those tents there flew the flag of the Purple Empire, with its grisly symbol of the severed head and the crossed broadswords.

These were the legions of the Purple Empire, ten strong divisions, which were tightening a cordon inexorably around Death Valley, where the American Army lay encamped.

By turning his head the sentry could look down into the long narrow strip of barren, parched land that was Death Valley. Here, in this valley, were a hundred thousand Americans, equipped with cannon, trucks, supplies and ammunition that they had captured from the Purple Empire.

Their encampment stretched along the valley for almost a hundred miles, and the sentry could see gun carriages and armored trucks. There were also, at frequent intervals, many tall skeleton-like structures each of which had a sort of pipe line poking out at its top. Those structures were the water towers, constructed by the American scientist, Franklin Ransom. It was

Ransom who had suggested that if the army would winter in Death Valley, he would undertake to provide water. And he had made good. Those towers were spouting water—water which kept life in the hundred thousand patriots here assembled.

At first upon hearing that the Americans had taken refuge in Death Valley, Marshal Kremer, the Commander of the Imperial Armies, had chuckled.

"They will come out soon," he said, "when they begin to burn with thirst. And then we will cut them to pieces. It is impossible for us to attack them in Death Valley; we could not scale the ridges of the mountain chains on either side. But we won't need to attack. They'll come out to us—and be glad to surrender in exchange for a drink of water!"

But a week had passed, and then two, and three; and no Americans came out to beg for water. It was then that Marshal Kremer understood that the Americans must have found a way to beat Death Valley. And in his rage, he threw ten crack divisions around the American Army. Then he sat down to wait. Sooner or later, they would come out. And Kremer was a bulldog who could wait a year if necessary.

Along the ridge here, there were a number of masked American batteries, ready to roar into action if the Purple division attacked. Thus far, however, there had been no hostile move on the part of the enemy.

A few miles up the Valley, the American flag stirred sluggishly in the hot breeze over G.H.Q. Within the tent sat General Hank Sheridan and Diane Elliot.

HANK SHERIDAN had started as the mayor of a small

Western town, who was among the first to organize opposition to the conquering cohorts of the Purple Empire. Since then he had demonstrated his innate military ability—an ability he had never suspected in himself—and had risen to high command in the American Defense Force. Unwilling to surrender with the rest of the Defense Force at the Rocky Mountains, he had cooperated with Operator 5 in leading this remnant of the American Armies into quarters in Death Valley; and while Operator 5 was gone, Hank Sheridan was in supreme command.

Diane Elliot faced him across the rude pine table in the tent, which served as a desk when they were not eating on it. Diane's chestnut hair was carelessly tucked in under a campaign hat, and her blouse was open at the throat to reveal the soft whiteness of her skin. She had been a newspaper woman before the invasion—and a little more than that, too. For she was one of that small, devoted band who took their orders from Operator 5. If she loved Jimmy Christopher, she had never let love interfere with his career, but had kept it well in the background. Beautiful, clever, accomplished, she had often helped Operator 5 in difficult and dangerous missions; and since the Purple Invasion she had fought almost constantly at his side.

Now these two, Hank Sheridan and Diane Elliot, were listening to a long series of words emanating from a short wave radio set alongside the table. They both wore earphones, and Diane was writing swiftly in longhand, while Hank Sheridan consulted a code book at his elbow. The voice that was reciting those words through the air was the voice of Operator 5. He was delivering orders to Hank Sheridan by code.

"Go to that telephone, Major Herbst!"

At last he finished. "Decode the foregoing orders, and execute at once. Keep me advised by radio of your progress. Will endeavor to time our movements accurately with yours. Good luck!"

The stiffness dropped from his voice as he finished, and he added softly: "Best wishes, Hank; and my love to Di. Tell her that Nan and Mac and Tim are all safe. Be seeing you soon!"

The radio became silent, and Diane looked up at Hank with glowing eyes. "It's coming, Hank—the Big Push! We're going into action!"

Hank Sheridan nodded soberly. "Wait'll I get this decoded."

He worked a while in silence, then turned the completed sheet around so she could read it too. "Whew! Jimmy is no piker. He's fixin' to attack Los Angeles!"

"Los Angeles!" Diane breathed. "Why, the Purple High Command considers it impregnable!"

Hank Sheridan shrugged. "But it would be swell if we could take the town. They've got immense stores there. We could put a million men in the field with the supplies they've got there!"

"But how are we going to get out of Death Valley? Kremer's shock troops are surrounding us—"

Hank grinned. "Jimmy doesn't say anything about that in the orders. He just says—*'March!'*—and it's up to us to march. We're to load every available truck, take every gun that can be moved, and advance against Los Angeles. He's coming up along the coast with the *Kondor,* and will shell the city just about the time we attack from land. It'll be sort of turning the tables on Kroner. That's the way he attacked us a few months ago. The only difference is that we only have a hundred thousand men now, against a couple of million!"

"Never mind," said Diane. "We'll do it!" She got up from the table. "I'm going up on Ridge Two, and take a look at the enemy's encampment. They're squatting right on the highway. Maybe I'll get an inspiration."

"I hope you do, Di. In the meantime, I'll give the orders to prepare to march. The boys'll like that. They're getting tired of sitting around here doing nothing, bottled up by the enemy like this. I bet they won't care *what* they have to march through, as long as they get moving!"

Diane nodded, and went out. She got in a staff car, and drove to Ridge Two, which overlooked the highway and the Mojave desert.

She climbed to the top of the ridge, thinking deeply. There must be some way to get through there—some way to fool the enemy. And get through they must, for they could not let Jimmy down!

AT THE top of the ridge, she paused for a moment to glance somberly down at the far-spreading camp of the enemy. There seemed to be a good deal of unusual activity down there. Motorized units were moving about in formation, and gun-carriages were being wheeled into place. Suddenly Diane thrilled. The enemy was going to attack!

She glanced around hastily in search of the sentinel who should be here. And abruptly she tensed.

There on the ground, less than twenty feet away from her, lay the bloody body of the sentry. He had been run through the back with a bayonet, and the ground was slowly encarmined with his blood. She saw at a glance that the man was dead.

Her eyes darted around in search of the perpetrator of this killing, and she kept her ears alert for the slightest sound.

She moved slowly, carefully, without making any noise. She passed the body of the sentry, stooped to touch his cold face to make sure he was dead; then she proceeded cautiously. Fifty feet further on she saw the men who had killed the sentry.

There were three of them—an officer and two troopers. The troopers were watching the officer, who was kneeling beside a field telephone, completing the connection. Manifestly, they were a scouting party, and they had strung this telephone up here to the ridge for the purpose of directing the advance of the troops.

Now, Diane could see a number of small groups of planes, far to the west. Those planes would constitute the advance guard of the enemy's attack. But now she paid no attention to the planes. She concentrated on that officer and his men.

In her absorption, she did not notice the single Purple Empire trooper who was stealing up quietly behind her. This trooper was a member of the patrol who had been sent to reconnoiter the other side of the ridge. Returning, he spied Diane. Now, he kept back, holding his rifle ready, smiling cruelly. He would wait, then pounce upon her.

Diane moved forward as quietly as possible, until she was within ten paces of the group. She took shelter behind a tree, and watched.

The officer finally grunted in satisfaction, and raised his head, then spoke into the telephone.

"Imperial Staff Headquarters!" he said. "This is Major Herbst, reporting on position of enemy. We are on ridge overlooking the valley. We have disposed of the sentry, and will be able to direct the troop movements without interference—"

Suddenly, the inspiration which Diane had been seeking came to her. Acting quickly, she withdrew the service revolver from the holster at her side, and stepped forward.

"Put your hands up—all of you!" she ordered crisply.

CHAPTER 10
LOS ANGELES OR BUST!

THE OFFICER jumped to his feet, his hand going to his holster. But he froze at the sight of the muzzle of Diane's gun peering at him. The two troopers stood dumb with amazement, gripping their heavy rifles.

"Raise your hands!" Diane repeated.

Major Herbst slowly complied. As he did so, a cunning gleam came into his eyes. He had glimpsed the trooper who was stealing up behind her, with the bayonet of his rifle gleaming in the sunlight. In a moment that trooper would be close enough to run her through the way the sentry had been "disposed of."

Diane noted the tense attitude of the major, as well as that of his two men, who had also glimpsed their fellow trooper. Her eyes narrowed. These men did not seem so despairing at being captured as they should. Something was wrong.

And just then, a twig snapped behind her.

In a flash she understood. She heard the heavy lumbering movement of the trooper at her back, and the muscles of her body reacted instantaneously to the impulse from her brain. She twisted to one side, and dropped prone on the ground, just as the trooper's bayonet flashed through the air in a vicious upward lunge that would have torn at her vitals had it found her.

The trooper stumbled, trying to regain his balance, and Diane fired upward once. The high-calibered bullet caught the man in the chin, smashed out through the top of his skull, clanging dully against his tin helmet, and lifting it into the air for almost an inch, in spite of the chin strap. The man was dead before his body landed on the ground, almost beside Diane.

She didn't wait to see him fall, but rolled over and over on the ground, twisted round to face the other three. The troopers were raising their rifles, and the officer's revolver was sliding out of its holster, gripped in his gloved hand.

Diane's lips clamped tight. She fired again and again, emptying the chamber of her revolver. Her first shot caught Major Herbst in the arm, spun him around, flinging the officer's gun twenty feet away. Her next shots were directed at the troopers. How many times she hit them she didn't know, but when the deafening explosions of her gun began to die away, both of them lay across their rifles, unmoving.

The officer was the only one of the patrol to remain alive. Diane's eyes flicked toward the spot where she had seen the dead body of the American sentry.

"That kind of squares things for you, buddy," she said softly.

Slowly she got up, keeping Major Herbst covered. And abruptly she realized that there were no more cartridges in her gun.

The major was pressing his wounded arm to his side, lips tight with the pain of his wound. But his small, ferret-like eyes were watching Diane like a hawk. There was a calculating gleam in them. She understood why.

He knew that her gun was empty!

Suddenly, he turned without a word, and began to run back toward the spot where his own revolver had fallen.

Diane thought and acted swiftly. She dropped to her knees, scooped up the rifle of the trooper who had fallen, and ran directly at the major, with the point of the bayonet flashing in the sunlight. She was younger than he, unwounded, lithe and active. Her feet pattered on the ground as she raced breathlessly to head him off. She reached the major just as he stooped for the gun.

Before he could touch the weapon, Diane thrust the bayonet out so that it touched his spine, the point pricking his tunic.

"As you were, Major!" she ordered.

Herbst snarled, took his hand away from the revolver. Diane goaded him away from it, stooped and picked it up herself.

HERBST WATCHED her closely. His arm was bleeding, and she saw the hate that lanced out at her from under his bushy eyebrows. It was a disgrace to be captured by a woman. He would never live this down in his officer's clubs.

She said to him tightly: "Get over to that telephone, Major Herbst!"

His eyes lit up with cunning. "You—want that I should speak to my headquarters?"

She nodded. "And you're going to tell them just what I tell you to tell them. Don't try to play any tricks, because I understand your language as well as you do!"

He moved over toward the field telephone. Sputtering sounds were coming from it. Headquarters must be wondering what had happened.

"Tell them that you were interrupted by an American, but that everything is all right now."

Herbst glared at her, but obeyed.

Diane held the gun at the back of his neck. "And now tell them that the American Army is moving out of Death Valley—out through Mono Lake and Tioga Pass, in the north!"

"But that is not so. They are not moving out through the north—"

Diane increased the pressure of the cold steel muzzle upon his neck. "Nevertheless, that is what you are going to tell them, *Herr* Major—if you do not wish to have your head blown off!"

The major hesitated. He covered the mouthpiece with his hand. "I understand your plan. You wish my headquarters to believe that you are escaping to the north. They will move all these troops away from here to cut you off; and then you will march out without opposition!"

"You're clever, Major. That is the plan."

"I will not do it! I will not betray my Emperor—"

"As you please, Major. When I count three, if you have not told them that, then I shall shoot."

Herbst swallowed hard.

Diane said: *"One!"*

Herbst swallowed again, his Adam's apple working up and down in ludicrous fashion.

"Two!"

Herbst weakened. Hastily he raised the telephone, spoke into it. "Major Herbst reporting. The Americans are leaving Death Valley. They are marching north, toward Mono Lake and Tioga Pass. I advise that all available troops be sent north to cut off the Americans!"

He spoke for several minutes longer, inventing details of the imaginary movements of the American Army. His imagination was spurred by the gun which Diane held at his neck. At last, he convinced his headquarters that he was not reporting a mirage. "I will call back as soon as I have further information."

He set down the instrument, turned to Diane, still nursing his wounded arm. "I have done what you asked. Now take me quickly to a doctor. I will bleed to death!"

Diane Elliot nodded. She tried to hide from him the relief that she felt. She would never have shot this man in cold blood if he had refused to betray his country. But, just as Flexner had allowed himself to be bluffed, this man, judging the Americans by himself, really believed that he would have been a dead man at the count of three. He himself would not have hesitated to treat a prisoner that way, and he could therefore believe it of the enemy.

Diane stepped back a pace, looked up into the western sky. The enemy planes were growing in number, approaching ever closer to Death Valley. Once they flew over the Valley, they would see that Herbst had not reported the truth. The plan would be ruined.

She backed away from Herbst, saying: "Follow me. I'll get you medical aid."

She moved back toward where the dead sentry lay. Glancing around, she found the field telephone with which the sentry had kept in touch with his commander. She made Herbst turn around with his back to her, and picked up the instrument. "Give me G.H.Q.—quick!" she rapped. In a moment she was talking to Hank Sheridan. She told him swiftly what had happened, what her plan was. "Get the Army ready, Hank. If the enemy moves out of here, we'll march at once. And for God's sake, get all the anti-aircraft guns in the valley to work. Keep a constant barrage of archie fire in the air. If a single one of the enemy planes flies over the Valley, the whole thing falls through!"

"You bet, Di!" Hank exclaimed. "The air'll be so thick with archie, those Purple flyers'll be damned glad to get back to their dromes. And they'll think we're just doin' it to cover our retreat toward the north!"

"Fine, Hank; and say, send up a stretcher for a wounded prisoner!"

She put down the phone, and stood up, keeping Herbst covered. The enemy planes were coming closer now, the roaring of their motors growing in crescendo. And almost at once, the anti-aircraft guns of the Americans began to spit and vomit flame. The air became filled with the noise and rattle of gunfire.

The enemy planes rode into the thick of it, and two were shot down before the others turned tail and fled.

The archie fire continued. Hank was taking no chances of even one enemy plane getting a view of the Valley.

Diane stood watching the enemy encampment for a long time. Once in a while she made Herbst get on the phone and give his headquarters further misleading information. At last, she breathed a deep sigh.

She saw a whole regiment of mechanized infantry, spread out on the desert ground below, fall into line and begin to march toward the north.

Other contingents fell into line behind them. The Purple Headquarters had fallen for the bait. They were marching to the north, and leaving the highway here defended by only a skeleton force. The Americans would win through easily.

Then the rest would be up to them!

They would reach the Los Angeles defenses fresh, without being exhausted by previous fighting. And there would be staged the decisive battle—the battle that would mean the rebirth of American independence, or death of the last hope of American freedom.

Trembling, Diane picked up the phone again. "Get started, Hank! The coast is clearing. Los Angeles or bust!" she said huskily.

CHAPTER 11
THE BATTLE OF LOS ANGELES

THE ROLLING thunder of great guns filled the air. The rattle of rifle fire and the chatter of machine guns mingled with the whine of whistling shells as men died, or screamed with the agony of wounds.

The Americans were assaulting the defenses around Los Angeles.

They had pushed through two hundred miles of hostile country, fighting their way through steady opposition. And now, in the foothills of the Santa Monica Mountains, they hit the defense line of fortifications built by the Purple Empire.

Marshal Kremer had been rushing these defenses to completion as fast as he could. Had this battle taken place three months later, the Americans would have stood no chance at all. But the pill-box-trench system of fortifications, which Kremer had planned to model along the idea of the old Maginot Line of France, was not yet fully complete at this time, and the Americans were staking everything on a desperate thrust here at the north, through the Santa Monica Mountains.

The advance was spread out along a wide front. Hank Sheridan's men were pushing on through the canyons, following river beds, winding roads, moving precariously along the crest of hills.

The Americans had had little time to lay down a barrage of their own, because they must win quickly, or not at all. Behind them, those ten divisions of Kremer's shock troops were marching swiftly to avenge the ruse that had been played upon them. Kremer had permitted himself to be fooled, for once.

On the crest of a hill, Hank Sheridan stood with Diane Elliot and several of his staff officers. Couriers were hurrying back and forth with messages.

Shells were screaming overhead, from two of the enemy batteries in Pasadena, but otherwise the Purple artillery was quiet.

Hank Sheridan was focusing his glasses on the vast stretch of land visible from this crest. The American boys were advancing successfully along a wide front, and Hank could see the gray uniforms spreading out and mopping up in several directions. He was jubilant, and he turned, threw his arms around Diane, and squeezed her hard.

"Girl!" he exclaimed, "we're close to victory! Hear those heavy guns to the west? Those are the guns of the *Kondor.* Jimmy Christopher is anchored out in Santa Monica Bay, and he has the range of the city. He's silenced most of the enemy batteries. Now, if he could only get those guns in Pasadena, everything would be jake!"

DIANE WAS thinking of this as she watched the Sepulveda Road, almost at their feet. It was along this road that the Americans would have to advance to take Los Angeles, and the troops were even now moving forward. This was the last spot where they could expect to encounter opposition. For here, at the Westwood end of the road, the enemy had erected a pillbox fortress, equipped with two eight-inch guns, and with a couple of machine guns. The pill-box was cleverly located under the brow of a hill, so that it was protected from the American artillery; nevertheless, it commanded the Sepulveda Road, and the Americans could not capture Los Angeles without taking that little fortress.

Now, as Diane watched, she saw the Americans advancing, saw the pill-box belch fire, saw the Americans begin to drop. They kept on, but the loss of life was too heavy. Abruptly, Hank Sheridan exclaimed: "God, I can't do it! I can't order them to die like that!" He raised his hand to his staff officer.

"Tracy! Order them to fall back!" He spread a map on the ground, bent over it. "We've got to find some other angle of attack," he told Diane. "We've got to take that pill-box. The longer we stay here, the closer Kremer's ten divisions will come. And if they catch us like this, our victory will turn into a defeat. We'll be—"

He broke off, staring at the bedraggled figure that approached them, accompanied by an American infantryman. At first he didn't recognize that figure. But Diane did.

"Jimmy!" she cried. She ran toward him, threw her arms around him. He was wearing the torn trousers of a Purple officer, but his tunic was gone, and his shirt was ripped. His shoulders and arms and hands were scratched and bleeding, but he was grinning.

Hank Sheridan came running over, while Jimmy Christopher clasped Diane tightly to him.

"My God, Operator 5!" he exclaimed. "What's happened to you?"

"I left Frank Ames in command of the *Kondor*," Jimmy told

him, "and came through the enemy lines to join you. When I got through, our own boys thought I was an enemy officer, and they started shooting at me, so I had to rip off my tunic. And then I hit a stretch of ground where the enemy had laid some barbed-wire, and I had a time getting across that."

"Well, thank God you've come!" Hank Sheridan breathed. "Because I'm at the end of my rope!" While one of Hank's staff officers went to get Jimmy a uniform, Hank quickly told him of the situation here. "That damned pill-box is the only thing that stands between us and Los Angeles," he finished. "If we could get past that—"

Jimmy nodded. "We could take the town easily. The *Kondor* has been raking the city with broadsides, and the enemy can't hold the town. Frank Ames is ready to put off a landing party, but he's got to be sure we'll meet him from this end. Let's take a look at that pill-box!"

"You see," Hank explained, "we can't lay down any artillery on it, and we can't get close to it by way of the road."

"I think there's a way," Jimmy said slowly, "if we could get a hundred men or so who aren't afraid to die."

One of the staff officers laughed bitterly. "A hundred! I could get you a thousand—ten thousand! Just say when you want them!"

"I want them now, Tracy," Operator 5 told him. "And get ten supply trucks. Load half a dozen barrels of explosive on the trucks. Bring them out on the road, and I'll join you."

"Explosive?" Tracy asked. "But the minute those trucks are hit, they'll go up—"

"That's right, Tracy. But one may get through the barrage. That'll be enough."

Tracy saluted. "I'll put T.N.T. on those trucks. They'll be ready in fifteen minutes."

"Make it ten minutes!" Jimmy Christopher said.

TEN MINUTES later he climbed down onto the Sepulveda Highway, to join the company of men lined up alongside ten huge army trucks. Tracy saluted, grinning. "Ten minutes is right, sir. And here are your hundred men. They're all ready to die—they've made their wills and everything!"

"Okay, Tracy," Jimmy swung to face the hundred volunteers. Swiftly he explained his plan. "Are you willing, boys?"

They raised their voices in a loud cheer. The plan he had outlined meant the death of perhaps ninety of them. But it would also mean an American victory. Their answer was a cheer.

In a few moments, the first of the trucks set off down the highway. They had gathered around a bend in the road, which was shielded from the pill-box. Once around that bend, the pill-box guns began to belch, spraying the road.

The trucks raced through the hail of fire. Number one was hit and careened off the side of the road. The driver, though he himself was struck by a bit of shrapnel, made sure to get the truck over to the side, so that those behind could pass.

The other trucks drove swiftly past, and number two was hit, a minute later, also swerved to one side, allowing number three to pass.

Jimmy Christopher, riding a motorcycle alongside number three, smiled grimly. He had accurately gauged the timing and firing frequency of the pill-box from the information that Hank Sheridan had given him. That pill-box had only two guns. Their crews fired simultaneously. And it took them precious time to put in fresh shells and fire.

Hank Sheridan, watching from the crest with Diane, stood tensely, his glasses glued to his eyes. "They're making it, Di!" he shouted wildly. "Five trucks down, but the others are within a couple of hundred yards—"

He broke off, uttered a groan. "Oh, God! They can't go any further. The road is broken up!"

"I see!" Diane whispered. "They—*they're going to charge on foot!*"

It was true. The surviving trucks were pulled up now to form a barricade in the road against the machine-gun fire which the enemy was now using at this close range. And from those trucks, the Americans with Jimmy Christopher in the lead, came running at double time. They spread out in wide formation, and Diane could see men falling at every step. Several of the men carried barrels of the T.N.T., and other men ran directly in front of them, so that enemy machine-gun bullets could not reach the barrels of explosive.

Jimmy Christopher in the lead came up to within ten feet of the pill-box, and hurled a grenade directly at the loophole through which one of the machine-guns was firing. The machine-gun was silenced. The Americans sent up a wild cheer, and covered the intervening distance to the door of the pill-box.

They set down the barrel of explosive, and ran in all directions. Jimmy Christopher, from a distance of almost a hundred yards, seized a rifle from one of the men, and took careful aim. He fired three times in quick succession, and the bullets slammed squarely into the barrel of explosive propped against the door.

There was the blinding flash of an explosion, and when the smoke cleared away the whole front of the pill-box was seen to have been blown away.

With a wild shout of victory the Americans charged. The road was filled with Hank Sheridan's men. The American advance was resumed!

With that pill-box out of the way, the capture of Los Angeles was an accomplished fact. Hank Sheridan's army of a hundred thousand men swarmed into the city, already partly subdued by the bombardment from the *Kondor*.

The first great step toward American Independence had been taken.

That night, Jimmy Christopher broadcast from KNX in Los Angeles.

"Citizens of America!" he said. "The first step has been taken. We have shown you that Americans still know how to fight. But there are not enough of us to fight this whole war. We need every man of you who can reach us. There are enough supplies here in Los Angeles to equip an army of a million men. The rest is up to you. Join us, Americans, for a free America. Directions as to how to contact recruiting agents will be broadcast later on short-wave sets, with distorters. The amateur radio stations in your neighborhood will spread the instructions. Let's see how Americans respond!"

When he finished his broadcast, he joined the small group that was waiting for him below. There were Nan and Mac, Diane and Tim, and Frank Ames and Hank Sheridan.

"It's up to us," he told them, "to lead America to victory. Now, everyone, chin up, and take your orders. There are busy days ahead for all of us, and, God willing, we'll drive the Purple Empire back into the ocean!" *

* Author's Note: After the capture of Los Angeles by the American troops under Operator 5, the vengeful troops of the Purple Empire, goaded on by their enraged, sadistic Emperor, ravaged and laid waste cities and towns throughout the country. So great was the destruction of natural resources that our citizens were reduced to the living conditions of primitive tribes. It was with this handicap against him that Operator 5 faced the task of welding together America's suffering millions into a unified movement against the ruthless Purple Emperor. And when the subtle intrigues of Baron Flexner's cunning mind were added to the complications of the situation, Operator 5 found that the road to liberty led almost to the brink of destruction. The fateful events of those troubled days will be recounted in detail for the first time, in the next novel from the pen of Curtis Steele, entitled "Drums of Destruction."

POPULAR HERO PULPS AVAILABLE NOW:

ACE G-MAN
☐ #1: The Suicide Squad Reports for Death $14.95

CAPTAIN COMBAT
☐ #1: The Sky Beast of Berlin $13.95
☐ #2: Red Wings For the Blood Battalion $13.95
☐ #3: Low Ceiling For Nazi Hell Hawks $13.95

OPERATOR 5
☐ #1: The Masked Invasion $13.95
☐ #2: The Invisible Empire $13.95
☐ #3: The Yellow Scourge $13.95
☐ #4: The Melting Death $13.95
☐ #5: Cavern of the Damned $13.95
☐ #6: Master of Broken Men $13.95
☐ #7: Invasion of the Dark Legions $13.95
☐ #8: The Green Death Mists $13.95
☐ #9: Legions of Starvation $13.95
☐ #10: The Red Invader $13.95
☐ #11: The League of War-Monsters $13.95
☐ #12: The Army of the Dead $13.95
☐ #13: March of the Flame Marauders $13.95
☐ #14: Blood Reign of the Dictator $13.95
☐ #15: Invasion of the Yellow Warlords $13.95
☐ #16: Legions of the Death Master $13.95
☐ #17: Hosts of the Flaming Death $13.95
☐ #18: Invasion of the Crimson Death Cult $13.95
☐ #19: Attack of the Blizzard Men $13.95
☐ #20: Scourge of the Invisible Death $13.95
☐ #21: Raiders of the Red Death $13.95
☐ #22: War-Dogs of the Green Destroyer $13.95
☐ #23: Rockets From Hell $13.95
☐ #24: War-Masters from the Orient $13.95
☐ #25: Crime's Reign of Terror $13.95
☐ #26: Death's Ragged Army $13.95
☐ #27: Patriots' Death Battalion $13.95
☐ #28: The Bloody Forty-five Days $13.95
☐ #29: America's Plague Battalions $13.95
☐ #30: Liberty's Suicide Legions $13.95
☐ #31: Siege of the Thousand Patriots $13.95
☐ #32: Patriots' Death March $14.95
☐ **NEW:** #33: Revolt of the Lost Legions $14.95

DUSTY AYRES AND HIS BATTLE BIRDS
☐ #1: Black Lightning! $13.95
☐ #2: Crimson Doom $13.95
☐ #3: The Purple Tornado $13.95
☐ #4: The Screaming Eye $13.95
☐ #5: The Green Thunderbolt $13.95
☐ #6: The Red Destroyer $13.95
☐ #7: The White Death $13.95
☐ #8: The Black Avenger $13.95
☐ #9: The Silver Typhoon $13.95
☐ #10: The Troposphere F-S $13.95
☐ #11: The Blue Cyclone $13.95
☐ #12: The Tesla Raiders $13.95

MAVERICKS
☐ #1: Five Against the Law $12.95
☐ #2: Mesquite Manhunters $12.95
☐ #3: Bait for the Lobo Pack $12.95
☐ #4: Doc Grimson's Outlaw Posse $12.95
☐ #5: Charlie Parr's Gunsmoke Cure $12.95

THE MYSTERIOUS WU FANG
☐ #1: The Case of the Six Coffins $12.95
☐ #2: The Case of the Scarlet Feather $12.95
☐ #3: The Case of the Yellow Mask $12.95
☐ #4: The Case of the Suicide Tomb $12.95
☐ #5: The Case of the Green Death $12.95
☐ #6: The Case of the Black Lotus $12.95
☐ #7: The Case of the Hidden Scourge $12.95

THE SECRET 6
☐ #1: The Red Shadow $13.95
☐ #2: House of Walking Corpses $13.95
☐ #3: The Monster Murders $13.95
☐ #4: The Golden Alligator $13.95

CAPTAIN ZERO
☐ #1: City of Deadly Sleep $13.95
☐ #2: The Mark of Zero! $13.95
☐ #3: The Golden Murder Syndicate $13.95